# Stars, Stripes, and Surprises

*A Molly Classic*
*Volume 2*

*by* Valerie Tripp

✭ American Girl®

*To Emily Stuart Matthewson*

*To Pleasant*

*To Katherine Helen Petty*

# Beforever™

The adventurous characters you'll meet in the BeForever books will spark your curiosity about the past, inspire you to find your voice in the present, and excite you about your future. You'll make friends with these girls as you share their fun and their challenges. Like you, they are bright and brave, imaginative and energetic, creative and kind. Just as you are, they are discovering what really matters: Helping others. Being a true friend. Protecting the earth. Standing up for what's right. Read their stories, explore their worlds, join their adventures. Your friendship with them will BeForever.

# TABLE *of* CONTENTS

| | | |
|---|---|---|
| 1 | Guess What? | 1 |
| 2 | The Blackout | 14 |
| 3 | The Princesses | 25 |
| 4 | Planning the Party | 34 |
| 5 | Yank and Bennett | 45 |
| 6 | Camp Gowonagin | 51 |
| 7 | We're in the Army Now | 67 |
| 8 | Creepy Crawlies | 80 |
| 9 | Victory at Sea | 90 |
| 10 | The Pink Army | 99 |
| 11 | Hurray for the U.S.A.! | 104 |
| 12 | A Hair-Raising Experience | 116 |
| 13 | The New Molly | 129 |
| 14 | The Show Must Go On | 140 |
| | Inside Molly's World | 156 |

# Guess What?

olly McIntire was skipping rope at the end of her driveway on a blustery afternoon in early spring. She was waiting for her friends Linda and Susan. Molly had a very important piece of news to tell them. Oh, wait until they heard! Molly skipped a little faster, as if that would make them come sooner. The wind sent high white clouds hurrying across the sky. It pushed hard against Molly, too, but she wouldn't budge from her lookout post. Where *were* Linda and Susan? Molly stopped skipping. She shaded her eyes and peered down the street. They were supposed to come over right after lunch. Molly felt as if she had been waiting forever.

At last Molly saw her friends. Linda was walking quickly. She bent into the wind. Her hands were shoved deep in her pockets. She stopped from time to time to wait for Susan, who was much slower. Susan had one foot on the curb and one foot in the gutter, where she was carefully cracking the thin ice over winter's last puddles.

"Hurry up!" Molly called. Linda poked Susan and they both ran to Molly.

"Guess what! Guess what!" shouted Molly as they came near.

"What?" Linda and Susan puffed together.

"An English girl is coming to stay with us!" said Molly happily.

"Oooh!" breathed Susan.

"What do you mean?" asked Linda.

"A girl," said Molly, "from London. Her parents want her to come to America, where it's safe. She's supposed to stay with her aunt here in Jefferson until the war's over. But her aunt has pneumonia or something and can't take her, so my mom said she could stay with us."

"Until the war's over?" asked Linda.

"No, just until her aunt gets better," said Molly. "But Mom said she'd be with us a couple of weeks at least, and that means she'll be here for my birthday."

"Oh, Molly," sighed Susan. "You're so lucky! A real English girl for your birthday!"

"I don't get it," said Linda. "Why is she coming *now*? It's 1944, and England has been in the war a long time."

"Well," Molly thought out loud, "maybe her house was just bombed by the Nazis."

"And she's probably raggy and starving like the children in *Life* magazine pictures," added Susan.

Linda shook her head. "Not everybody in England is ragged and starving, Susan," she said. "For all you know, she's as rich as a princess."

"A princess!" said Susan joyfully.

"I bet she even looks like one of the English princesses, Margaret Rose or Elizabeth!" said Molly. "I bet she has dark curly hair and blue eyes. She's going to share my room and come to school with me. She's exactly our age."

"Does she know your dad in England?" asked Linda.

"No, I don't think so," answered Molly. Molly's dad was a doctor who was in England helping sick and wounded soldiers.

"When does she come?" asked Susan.

"Today!"

"Today!" shrieked Susan and Linda. "What time?"

"Mom said before dinner," Molly answered.

"Well, I'm not going to stand out here all day waiting for her," said Linda. She was holding her coat collar up around her ears. "I'm cold. Let's go inside."

"Maybe when the English girl is here, Mrs. Gilford will give us little tea sandwiches every afternoon, like they have in England," said Susan dreamily.

"Maybe," said Molly. "Oh, it's going to be so much fun!"

"Will you two come on?" said Linda. She led the way to the house.

The three girls raced inside, through the bright kitchen, and down the stairs to the basement. Their new hideaway was in the corner next to Dad's workbench. They had set up a card table there and draped an old blanket over it. It was their pretend bomb shelter. A few Saturdays ago, when they went to the movies, they saw a newsreel that showed the different kinds of bomb shelters people used in England. One bomb shelter was a steel table with sides that rolled down. The sides were made of metal links. The table was set up in a living room. The newsreel showed a family rushing to get under the table at the sound of a warning siren. It seemed almost like a game, the same idea as musical chairs.

The girls had been very impressed. Imagine having a bomb shelter right in your own living room! It was horrifying and exciting at the same time. They had gone straight to Molly's house after the movies and made a pretend bomb shelter of their own. They liked to sit under the blanket-covered table and play that the house was collapsing around them. It was pleasantly scary.

"It smells like mothballs in here," complained Linda as she crawled under the table. "Do we have to have this old blanket over the table all the time?"

"Yes!" said Molly. "Remember the newsreel? When the bombs came, the people got under the table and rolled the sides down so they wouldn't get hurt."

"But those sides were like a fence," said Linda. "They had holes so you could at least breathe."

"Well, a blanket is the best we can do," said Molly. "Let's just play."

"Maybe the English girl has a bomb shelter just like this in her house in England," said Susan as she twisted the top off Molly's Girl Scout canteen. They kept the canteen full of water in case they decided to stay in their shelter for a long time. They wanted to keep crackers there, too, but Mrs. Gilford thought cracker crumbs would bring ants.

"Do you think English people ever stay in bomb shelters overnight?" asked Linda. "It's so crowded in here."

"I think sometimes they do," said Molly. She tried to straighten her legs, but there wasn't enough room under the table. "They have to stay in as long as the bombing goes on. Because if they came out too soon, something might fall on them, like bricks or a building or—"

WHAM! Something heavy landed right above their heads. The table wobbled. BAM! The table was struck again.

"Bombs away!" they heard.

The girls looked at each other and giggled. "Ricky!"

Molly lifted the blanket and stuck her head out. Ricky was bouncing his basketball on top of the table.

"Don't do that!" Molly said. She didn't mind very much, though, because the thud of the basketball made it easy to pretend there were real bombs outside.

"Some bomb shelter," said Ricky. "This wouldn't last two seconds if a real bomb fell. Don't you girls know anything? Real bomb shelters are outside, dug into the ground like caves." He bounced the ball on the table again.

"This is like what they have in England," protested Molly.

"Like fish it is," scoffed Ricky.

"It is, too," said Susan from inside. "We saw it at the movies."

"Where? In the cartoon?" asked Ricky.

"You wait, Ricky," said Molly. "Wait till the English girl comes. She'll tell you about bomb shelters."

Ricky groaned. "Just what I need," he said. "Another dippy girl around." But Molly noticed he didn't say anything more about their bomb shelter.

Ricky had just left when Molly's mother called down the stairs. "Girls? Come up here, please."

"She's here!" squealed Molly. "The English girl!" The three girls tumbled over each other struggling to be the first one out of their bomb shelter. They pounded up the stairs and into the kitchen. Molly stopped so suddenly that Susan stumbled into her back.

There, standing by the kitchen table, was the English girl. Mrs. McIntire was standing behind her, with her hands on the girl's shoulders. "Emily," she said, "I'd like you to meet Molly. Molly, this is Emily Bennett." Very gently, she pushed Emily toward Molly. Emily kept her eyes on the floor.

Molly held out her hand and smiled at Emily. "Hi," she said.

Emily glanced up at Molly, then looked down again. She touched Molly's hand with icy fingertips, whispered "How do you do," and stepped backward toward Mrs. McIntire.

Susan pushed past Molly. "How do you do?" she said. She pulled the sides of her pants legs as if they were the wide skirt of a ball gown and bobbed down in a curtsy. "I'm Susan," she said as she rose awkwardly. "I thought English girls always curtsied."

Ricky snorted and Molly and Linda giggled at Susan. Emily didn't look up, but Molly saw that her ears turned pink with embarrassment. *She thinks we're laughing at her,* Molly thought.

Molly moved toward Emily. "This is Linda," she said. "And here's Ricky, my brother. He's twelve. I have another brother named Brad, who is four, and a sister named Jill. She's fourteen. You'll meet them later."

Everyone was quiet, staring at Emily. Then Mrs. McIntire said, "We're very glad you're here, Emily. You'll get used to the names and faces soon." She patted Emily's shoulders. "Ricky, would you carry the suitcase upstairs, please? Molly, why don't you show Emily your room." She smiled and said, "It's going to be your room, too, Emily, for as long as you stay with us."

A very quiet parade climbed up the stairs. Ricky was in the lead, with Emily following. Molly, Linda, and Susan lagged behind. Linda whispered to Susan, "She's awfully little. And she sure doesn't look like a princess."

But Susan's eyes were glowing. "Of course she's little. Didn't I tell you she'd be starving?"

Emily was the skinniest girl Molly had ever seen.

Her knee socks were twisted and saggy around her legs, which were as thin as spaghetti noodles. Even her hair was skinny. It was gingery-red and absolutely straight. Her eyes were pale blue. Her skin was pale, too, as if she had not been outside in the sunshine for a very long while.

Ricky put Emily's suitcase on one of the beds in Molly's room and left. Linda and Susan flopped onto the other bed. "Well, here we are," said Molly. "Want me to help you unpack?"

Emily shook her head no. She stood by the door.

"Here," said Molly, "I'll make some room for your stuff in this chest." She scooped up a messy armful of socks from one drawer and shoved them into another. "You can have this whole drawer," she said.

Emily opened her suitcase. Carefully she lined up three pairs of socks, some underwear, and two pairs of pajamas in the drawer.

"Is that all you have?" asked Susan. "Did all your clothes get lost or burned up or something?"

Emily didn't answer. She was hanging two skirts and a white blouse in Molly's closet. She put the blouse on the hanger and buttoned up all the buttons. She folded the collar and moved the shoulders so that they were exactly straight on the bony skeleton of the hanger. "Well, we have lots of clothes and things you can use, so don't worry," Susan added.

Emily put her suitcase under the bed and smoothed the bedspread. "You sure like things neat," said Molly. She couldn't think of anything else to say. Emily seemed to have a wall around her that made her difficult to talk to. Then Molly thought of something Emily would be familiar with, something she could certainly talk about. "Come on, Emily," she said. "We have something to show you down in the basement."

"Oh, yeah," said Susan. "You'll like this."

Molly led the girls back downstairs. Emily walked stiffly, as if she were cold. When they got to the basement, she moved even more slowly. Molly pointed to the bomb shelter. "See?" she said. "It's a bomb shelter, like you have in England. We play in it all the time." She lifted the edge of the blanket and showed Emily the dark space under the table. "Want to go in?" she asked. "Come on. It's fun."

But Emily backed away from the bomb shelter. "No," she said. "No thank you. I'd rather not." Then she turned and walked quickly back up the stairs.

Molly, Susan, and Linda watched her go. "At least she finally said something," said Linda.

Molly sighed.

"You'd better go up and try to talk to her," said Susan. "You're supposed to be making friends with her, right?"

"Right," said Molly. She climbed slowly up the stairs to the kitchen. Mrs. McIntire was sweeping the kitchen floor.

"Are you looking for Emily?" she asked. "She said she was going upstairs to write a letter to her parents."

Molly wasn't sure what to do. "Do you think I should go up there?" she asked her mother.

Mrs. McIntire bent over to sweep under the kitchen table. "Why don't you leave Emily in peace for a while," she said. "She's probably feeling rather over-whelmed. She's had a big day."

"She's awfully quiet, isn't she?" said Molly. "She never says anything."

Mrs. McIntire straightened and chuckled. "Not everybody is a chatterbox like you are, olly Molly. English children are taught to be reserved—to be

very polite and quiet. Emily probably feels shy."
Mrs. McIntire swept the dirt into a dustpan. "Think
how you'd feel your first day with a brand-new
family."

"It seems as if she doesn't like us," said Molly.
"She won't smile or anything, and she wouldn't play
in the bomb shelter either."

Mrs. McIntire put the dustpan down and thought
for a moment. "Give Emily a chance, Molly. Remember, bomb shelters haven't been places for her to play.
In fact, the whole world must have seemed cold and
dangerous to Emily for a long time. The war in England has been going on since she was five—practically
her whole life. I think Emily is like a little crocus who's
not sure it's spring yet. It will take some time for her
to realize it's safe to come out now." She grinned at
Molly. "I imagine quite soon I'll have two chatterboxes
on my hands. But meanwhile, you be as warm and
friendly and welcoming as you can be to Emily, okay?"

"Okay, Mom," said Molly.

"That's my girl," said Mom.

Mom made it sound easy to make friends with
Emily. Molly wasn't sure it would be.

# The Blackout

olly did her best to make friends with Emily in the next few days, but she didn't get very far. Emily was always polite, but she never seemed to warm up. Molly tried everything. She showed Emily her most treasured possession—her nurse doll, Katharine. Molly's dad had sent Katharine to Molly as a Christmas present. Molly was sure Emily would see that Katharine was the most beautiful doll in the world.

"You see," Molly said as she handed the doll to Emily, "Katharine is dressed like a real English nurse."

"A nurse?" said Emily. "I don't think so."

"What do you mean?" Molly asked. "She comes from England. My dad sent her. And he said she's dressed like the nurses who work in the hospital with him."

Emily straightened Katharine's cap and said politely but firmly, "In England nurses take care of little children. Women who work in hospitals are called sisters. Your doll is dressed like a sister."

"No kidding!" said Molly. "That's great! I've always liked to pretend Katharine is my sister, and now it turns out she really is!"

Emily looked confused. She never understood when Molly said something silly just to be funny. "She isn't *your* sister. She's *a* sister," Emily said.

"Oh, well," said Molly. "Whatever you call her, she's beautiful, isn't she?"

"Very nice," said Emily coolly. She handed the doll back to Molly.

The first day Emily came to school, all the girls asked her lots of questions. They loved her English accent. "She sounds like a movie star, the way she says 'how do you do' and 'rah-ther,'" said Alison Hargate.

All morning long, everyone tried to imitate the way Emily talked. Emily herself didn't say very much. At lunch, Molly sat next to Emily. She tried to include her in the conversation. During recess, Susan asked, "Was your house ever bombed, Emily?"

Emily said, "No."

Susan kept on. "Did you ever see other houses being bombed?" she asked.

Emily didn't answer right away. Finally, she said, "Yes." Everyone waited for her to say more.

"Well? What was it like?" asked Linda. "Was it exciting?"

Emily looked frosty. "I don't remember," she said.

"Gosh, how could you forget a thing like that?" asked Susan.

Emily shrugged.

There was a chilly silence. Finally, Molly said, "Come on! Let's play jump rope." They all moved into the sunshine.

After a few days, everyone more or less ignored Emily at school. She was so quiet it was an easy thing to do. No one said it, but everyone thought Emily was a disappointment.

"Well, at least she's not a showoff," Linda pointed out. "I was afraid she'd expect all of us to make a fuss over her. I thought she might be stuck-up, but she's not."

"No," sighed Molly. "She's nice enough, I guess. She's just so . . ."

"Quiet," whispered Linda. Everyone giggled.

The girls were walking home from school under trees that were green with new buds. It was one of those tricky spring days that starts as winter in the morning and ends up as summer in the afternoon. Molly had her sweater tied around her waist. Susan had her jacket completely unbuttoned and her arms out of the sleeves. She was only wearing the hood, so the rest flapped behind her like a cape. Linda was the only one still wearing rubbers and a hat.

"Emily even brushes her teeth quietly," said Molly.

"Where is she now?" asked Susan.

"Mom is taking her to see her aunt in the hospital. Then they're going shopping. She has to get some sneakers, only she calls them 'plimsolls.' It's one of her weird English words."

"Plimsolls?" said Linda. She pinched her nose and said in a hoity-toity voice, "Oh, deah! My plimsolls smell simply dreadful."

"I don't think that's very nice, Linda," said Susan. "Did you ever think that maybe Emily is quiet because she doesn't like sounding so different? Or maybe it's because she doesn't know the American words for things. Of course, I still think she's quiet because she's weak and starving. She needs food."

"Mom gives her plenty of food," said Molly. "But she likes strange things like sardines. She doesn't like normal things like cake."

They all tried to imagine not liking cake.

"What kind of cake are you going to have at your birthday party?" asked Susan.

"Mrs. Gilford is going to make that vanilla cake without eggs or butter or milk. She's saved enough sugar rations and chocolate to make frosting," said Molly.

"Yummm," said Susan. "My favorite. If Emily doesn't want her piece, I'll eat it."

"Okay," laughed Molly, "we'll share it."

"Talking about cake makes me want some right now," said Susan. "Let's go see if Mrs. Gilford has any."

But Mrs. Gilford said it was too close to dinner-time for any snack other than carrot sticks, so the girls munched their way down to the bomb shelter to play.

Emily and Mrs. McIntire came home just as the rest of the family was sitting down to dinner. "The days are getting longer," Mrs. McIntire said cheerfully. "Spring is here. Doesn't someone in this family have a birthday in the spring?" she asked with a smile.

"I do!" said Molly. "My birthday is only a few weeks away."

"Have you decided what kind of party you want this year?" asked her mother.

"I haven't decided yet," said Molly. "I've been thinking about it and—"

Suddenly, a loud, shrill siren screeched.

"Hurray!" said Ricky. "A blackout!" He jumped up from the table. Emily shrank back in her seat.

"Oh, dear," sighed Mrs. McIntire. "A surprise blackout. All right, everyone, let's get going. Jill, you close the blackout curtains. Ricky, turn off all the lights. Molly and Emily, you take Brad downstairs. I'll get some blankets and be right down."

Molly was halfway to the stairs with Brad when she realized Emily wasn't following her. She was sitting at the table, as still as a stone.

"Come on, Emily," said Molly. "Hurry up!"

Emily didn't move.

Molly spoke louder. "Emily, you can't just sit there. It's a blackout. We all have to go downstairs. We have to hurry."

"Don't be scared, Emily," said Brad. "No bombs will come. This is only pretend."

Molly looked hard at Emily. Was Brad right? Was that the problem? Was Emily scared? She certainly looked scared. Her face was white. Molly's voice softened. "It's okay, Emily," she said. "It's just practice, really. I promise."

Emily didn't say anything. But she got up from the table and followed Molly downstairs.

"We have these blackouts every once in a while," Mrs. McIntire said to Emily when everyone was gathered in the basement. "They're a drill for us. There's not much chance of being bombed here, but we want to be ready just in case. So we practice turning out all the lights in town, so no one could see our houses from an airplane. But I imagine you know all about blackouts."

Emily was sitting in the darkest corner of the basement, a little apart from everyone else. Even though it wasn't cold, Emily was wrapped up in a blanket. Molly went over to sit next to her. She couldn't see Emily's face.

"Sometimes they tell us beforehand about the blackouts. Then Mom makes a thermos bottle of hot chocolate . . ." Molly stopped. She saw that Emily was shivering. "Emily? Are you okay?" she asked.

Emily sniffed. Molly realized she was crying. "What's the matter? Are you scared?"

Emily shook her head no. "I hate this," she said suddenly. Molly sat very still and listened. "I hate sitting in the dark, waiting. In England, back during the Blitz, almost every night we had to do this. You'd hear an awful noise, then one split second of silence, and then the explosion." Emily shuddered. "The whole house would shake. If we were on the street when the siren went off, we'd have to make a dash for the tube station—the subway, you call it. We sometimes had to sleep there, with all the other people, all crowded together."

Molly didn't know what to say.

Emily went on. "But it was almost worse afterward, coming out again. A house you'd walked past every day would be nothing but a pile of stones. Sometimes the flowers would still be growing along a path, and the path would lead to nothing. The house would be gone."

Emily pulled the blanket tighter. "In England the bombing isn't exciting at all. It isn't a game. It's terrible. People and . . . things get hurt. They get killed. You Americans don't know."

Molly waited to be sure Emily was finished talking. Then she said, "I guess we really don't know. We're safe here. And now you're safe, too, Emily."

Emily sighed. "But my mum and dad are still there."

Molly moved closer to Emily. She knew how it felt to be worried about someone far away and in danger. "My dad's there, too," she said. "I miss him so much my heart hurts."

Emily looked sideways at Molly. "Sometimes I feel like a coward to have left London."

"Oh, no," said Molly. "I think you're very brave to have been in the bombing. You're as brave as a soldier. You're the bravest person I know, after my dad."

"If I were really brave, I would have asked my

parents to let me stay," Emily said sadly.

Molly wanted to make Emily feel better. "But even the princesses of England had to leave London," she said. "I read it in a magazine. They've moved out of the palace in London and out to . . . what's the name of that place?"

"Windsor Castle," said Emily.

"That's right," said Molly. "I read that they sleep in the dungeons every night, to be safe from bombs. They're very brave and they left London. You are just as brave as those princesses, Emily."

Emily let the blanket fall away from her head. "Do you like Princess Elizabeth and Princess Margaret Rose, too?" she asked.

"Oh, yes!" said Molly. "I always love to see them in the newsreels and magazines. I think they're so pretty. I even have paper dolls of them."

"You do?" said Emily. Her face looked bright. "I have a scrapbook full of their pictures. I even have pictures of them when they were little girls."

"Ohhh, how wonderful," said Molly. "Did you bring your scrapbook with you?"

"Yes!" said Emily. "It's in my bag, under my bed."

"Could I see it?" Molly asked eagerly.

"Of course!" said Emily.

Just then the all-clear signal blew and the blackout was over. Molly stood up. "Let's go," she said.

Emily gathered the blanket in her arms. "Yes, indeed," she said.

Molly grinned. And Emily actually smiled back.

# The Princesses

oth the princesses are Girl Guides. That's like your Girl Scouts," Emily was saying. "Here's a picture of them in their uniforms." Molly and Emily were in their room. They were looking at Emily's scrapbook filled with pictures of Princess Elizabeth and Princess Margaret Rose. A clean spring breeze puffed the curtains. Molly was sprawled on the floor on her stomach. Emily was sitting up with her back straight against Molly's bed. Emily always sat up straight. She never sprawled. She never took up too much room. But she wasn't stiff and silent anymore. Spring buds were opening up in the sunshine and Emily was, too.

Emily went on, "Of course, the princesses are practically grown-up ladies now. When they were our age, they used to wear matching clothes like this." She pointed to an old picture of the princesses in matching dresses. They were playing the piano together. A dog was lying asleep at their feet.

"We could do that!" said Molly. She jumped up and flung open the closet door. "We could dress alike, just as the princesses did. We could wear outfits that look like theirs, too. Wouldn't that be fun?"

Emily looked up at Molly. Her eyes were as blue as robins' eggs. Emily didn't say anything, but Molly now knew that when Emily was quiet, it did not mean she didn't care. Emily just didn't say everything she was thinking, the way Molly did when she got excited.

Molly rattled on. "See?" she said. "You have a blue skirt and so do I. That's just the kind of thing the princesses would wear. And we both have white blouses and blue sweaters . . ."

"You could borrow a pair of my blue knee socks," said Emily.

"Okay!" said Molly. "Come on! Let's put these clothes on."

Molly was dressed in a flash. She watched as Emily carefully buttoned her sweater all the way up to her chin. "How come you always button every button?" she asked Emily.

"I keep forgetting how warm your houses are here," said Emily. "In England houses are much colder."

"Even Windsor Castle?" asked Molly.

"Yes," nodded Emily. "Especially castles. The princesses have to make sacrifices because of the war. Their rooms are cold. They can put only a few inches of hot water in the bathtub. They even have to eat dreadful things like parsnips and turnips."

"Turnips!" said Molly. "We have to eat those here!"

Emily smiled. "You see, you're like the princesses, too. Did you ever think that your name starts with M like Margaret Rose—"

"And your name starts with E like Elizabeth," finished Molly.

The girls smiled at each other in the mirror. "Before you came here, I thought you might look like Princess Elizabeth," Molly said to Emily.

Emily grinned. "I rather expected you to look like Shirley Temple, the film star!" she said. "You know, big brown eyes and blond ringlets!"

Molly lifted her braids so that they stuck straight out of her head. "Not exactly blond ringlets. More like long brown sticks," she said.

"I think your hair is very nice, just as it is," said Emily.

"Well, it sure doesn't help me look like a movie star or a princess," sighed Molly. "Of course, if I really wanted to be like one of the princesses, I would have to get a dog. The princesses always have dogs with them, don't they?"

Emily bent over to pull up her knee sock.

"We'll just have to pretend we have dogs," said Molly. She snapped her fingers and said, "Here, boy!" She pretended to pat a dog at her feet. "Good dog!"

Emily looked down at the imaginary dog.

"Let's go for a walk," said Molly. "Don't forget your dog, Em—I mean Elizabeth." She led the way out of the room.

They bumped into Ricky in the hall. When he saw the girls, Ricky smirked. "Why are you two dressed alike?" he said in a disgusted voice. "It makes you look twice as drippy as usual. What stooges!"

Molly put her nose in the air. "Ignore him, Emily," she said. "He only wants attention."

But Emily was staring at the poster Ricky was

tacking to his door. It showed fighter planes from different countries. Ricky had cut the pictures out of magazines and labeled them all. "That one's wrong," Emily said quietly.

"What?" said Ricky.

"That plane," said Emily. She pointed to a small picture in the corner. "You've labeled it an enemy plane, but it isn't at all. It's an American plane. I'm sure."

Molly crowed with laughter. "Who's a stooge now, Ricky?" she asked.

"Huh!" said Ricky. He crossed his arms on his chest and looked at Emily. "What does a girl know about fighter planes anyway?"

"Oh, I've seen hundreds of fighter planes flying over England," said Emily.

"You have?" asked Ricky. He had never seen a single one.

"Of course," Emily said patiently. "Look here. See these white bands over the nose and the tail? That's what tells you it's an American plane. Besides—" she squinted at the blurry picture— "if you look very hard, you can tell that's a star, not a swastika, there near the tail. All the American planes have stars on them."

"I know *that*," snapped Ricky. He frowned at the poster and started to take it down. Without turning around he said, "Do you see any other mistakes?"

"Not right off," Emily said airily. "I'll look more carefully later though. Molly and I are going for a walk now." She and Molly floated down the hall, down the stairs, and outside.

It had rained during the night, and the girls had to skirt around mud puddles as they strolled along dragging their jump ropes. They were using the jump ropes as leashes for their imaginary dogs. Molly had a fine time pretending her dog was frisky.

"No, no!" she said. "Don't go in that puddle! Bad dog!" Molly yanked her jump rope through the water. Then she pretended to trip. She giggled, "Ooops! My dog twisted the leash around my legs! This is fun, isn't it?"

"Mmmhmm," Emily answered in her usual soft-spoken way. Her dog seemed to be well behaved and as quiet as Emily was herself.

"Of course, it would be better if we had real dogs," said Molly. "Do you like dogs, Emily?"

Emily's eyes were shining. "Oh, yes," she said. "I love dogs."

"Me, too," said Molly. "I think puppies are cute. And dogs are so much fun to play with."

"Yes," said Emily.

"Even before I was a princess, I wished I had a dog," Molly went on. "A dog can really be your friend. Don't you think so?"

But Emily didn't answer. Her imaginary dog must have tugged on its leash because Emily quickly moved a few steps ahead of Molly.

During the next few days, Molly and Emily took their imaginary dogs for a walk every afternoon. Everyone in the family got used to seeing them in their matching princess outfits, dragging their jump rope leashes and playing with their invisible dogs. The two girls liked to share Molly's roller skates, each wearing one, and skate down the sidewalk pretending their dogs were running behind.

"It's too bad we can't get a pair of skates for you," said Molly to Emily one afternoon. "But they're not making skates because of the war."

"Oh, I don't mind," said Emily cheerfully.

"Remember, we're princesses, and princesses never complain about the sacrifices they have to make."

Molly joked, "I wonder if the princesses ever skated with their dogs? I bet there's lots of room to skate in Windsor Castle."

They giggled as they skated up the driveway.

Mrs. McIntire was kneeling in the flower garden. She was pulling dead leaves away from some daffodils that were beginning to bloom. "Hello, your highnesses," she said. "What's all the giggling about?"

"We were thinking about skating in a palace," said Molly.

"I wish you would think about what kind of birthday party you'd like to have. It's less than a week away, you know," Mrs. McIntire said to Molly.

"I know," said Molly. "I just can't decide. I was thinking of going to the movies, but we did that last year. I want to do something different."

"How do you celebrate birthdays, Emily?" Mrs. McIntire asked.

Emily thought a moment. "In England, we used to have a tea party and—"

"A tea party!" Molly broke in. "Oooh! That's perfect!

Can we do that for my birthday, Mom?"

"I don't see why not," said Mrs. McIntire. "Emily can tell us exactly what to do."

Emily glowed. "Of course, I haven't actually had a big birthday party in a long time. Not since the war started, really, because it's impossible to get sweets and special foods," she added quickly. "But when I was much younger, I had a party with ten girls. The room was decorated with flowers and ribbons, and we played games and ate lovely treats."

"Like princesses!" said Molly. "That's what my birthday party will be: the princesses' tea party!" Then Molly had a wonderful idea. "Emily, why don't you share my birthday with me? It will make up for the parties you've missed. We'll have a tea party, and we'll be the princesses, you and me. We'll dress up so we'll look alike and everything. It will be the most wonderful birthday party anyone ever had. What do you think?"

Emily's cheeks were as pink as posies. "I think it would be very nice indeed," she said.

Molly knew that was an excited answer, coming from Emily. Emily must be very, very pleased, just as pleased as Molly was herself.

# Planning the Party

he very next day, Molly and Emily wrote out the invitations to their shared birthday party. Emily showed Molly the proper way to word the invitations.

"You see," Emily said, "in England we do invitations like this." Emily pushed her wispy hair behind her ears, hunched over the paper, and wrote

*Mrs. James McIntire requests*
*the honour of your presence at a tea*
*to celebrate the birthdays of*
*Miss Molly McIntire and Miss Emily Bennett*
*Saturday, the twenty-second of April*
*four o'clock at her home*

"That's wonderful!" said Molly. "It's so English."

Emily smiled.

"The only thing is, I'm a little worried because I don't think any of my friends really drink tea," said Molly. "So probably we should have cocoa instead."

Emily said slowly, "In England it's always real tea. I suppose you could put lots of hot milk and honey in the tea so that your friends will like it."

"I guess so," said Molly. "Usually at birthday parties we have cold milk with peanut butter sandwiches or hot dogs. Of course, at Alison Hargate's party we had ginger ale."

Emily shook her head. "In England we have tea sandwiches, not peanut butter or hot dogs. Tea sandwiches are very thin, not like American sandwiches. And the crusts are cut off."

"Well, that sounds okay," said Molly. "What's in the sandwiches?"

"Meat paste or watercress," said Emily.

"Meat paste?" asked Molly. "What's that?"

Emily explained. "It's a paste sort of like peanut butter, only it's made out of ground-up meat. Maybe ham or liver."

"Liver?" said Molly, horrified. "I don't think my

friends will like that."

Emily sighed. "I suppose we could have just bread and butter . . ."

"Butter is rationed," said Molly. "It will have to be bread and margarine."

"Very well," said Emily.

"Anyway," said Molly, "everyone mostly just eats the ice cream and cake at a birthday party."

"In England we don't have ice cream at tea," said Emily.

"No ice cream? Not even when it's a birthday tea party? You just have plain old cake?" Molly asked.

"Oh, no, indeed!" said Emily. "Not *plain* cake. At a tea party you'd have something special. Let's see," she thought. "It's not proper to have treacle pudding at tea. You'd have little cakes or a tart. Yes, I think probably a tart. A lemon tart."

"Wait a minute," said Molly. She wasn't absolutely sure what a lemon tart was, but she didn't like the sound of it. "Are you saying we'll have a lemon tart instead of a regular cake?"

Emily said, "Yes."

"But—but what do you put the candles in?" Molly

sputtered. "And what do you write Happy Birthday on?"

Emily didn't answer.

"Listen, Emily," said Molly. "My very favorite birthday thing, I mean what I myself like the best, is a big layer cake. It's not a birthday without a cake. And Mrs. Gilford has even saved enough of our cocoa ration for chocolate frosting this year. I know you'll like it." Emily didn't say anything, so Molly went on, "Maybe we could make the cake look English. We could make it in the shape of a castle or something . . ." Her voice trailed off. The two girls sat in stony silence.

At last Molly said, "What if we have an American cake, but all the rest of the food is English?"

"Then it wouldn't be a proper English princesses' tea at all," said Emily.

"Yes, it would," said Molly.

"No," said Emily briskly, "it would not."

"Okay, okay," said Molly. "As long as you're sure that's what the princesses would have."

"Oh, yes," said Emily. "I'm sure."

"Then let's go tell Mom about the food," Molly said to Emily. But to herself she said, *Margarine sandwiches,*

*milky tea, and a lemon tart. Maybe this tea party was not*
*such a hot idea after all.*

But all the girls at school thought the tea party
sounded absolutely wonderful. All week long, while
they were playing jump rope and dodgeball and hop-
scotch in the fresh spring sunshine, all anyone talked
about was "Emily's tea party."

"How simply elegant!" gushed Susan. "It's so
grown-up! I've never had real tea before!"

"You are so lucky, Molly," said Alison Hargate.
"Emily can tell you just how everything is done in
England."

Everyone envied Molly so much that she began to
think she really must be lucky. No one else seemed to
think a lemon tart was so bad.

By the night before the party, Molly and Emily both
felt jittery with excitement as they blew up balloons
and made party hats.

"Hey, Emily," said Molly. "We'd better not forget
to make crowns for ourselves."

"Crowns?" asked Emily.

"Sure, so everyone will know we're the princesses," said Molly. "I think I have two long dress-up dresses we can wear."

Emily laughed softly. "Oh, Molly, you're thinking of fairy-tale princesses. Princess Elizabeth and Princess Margaret Rose wear normal clothes."

"But I've seen pictures of them in crowns and long dresses," said Molly stubbornly. "Remember? There's a picture like that in your scrapbook."

"That picture was taken when their father was crowned the King of England," said Emily. "They don't wear those clothes for a tea party."

"Oh," said Molly. She had imagined herself curtsying deep into a billow of skirt. "Well, at least I have a nice party dress from last year."

"In fact, since it's a wartime party, the princesses would probably wear skirts and jumpers—you call them sweaters," said Emily. "They'd dress just as usual."

This was too much. "I'm not wearing boring old school clothes to my birthday party," Molly stated flatly. "All the other girls will have on their party dresses."

"The princesses—" Emily began.

"I don't care," said Molly. "I'm going to wear my party dress and that's final."

"But then we won't look like the princesses," said Emily.

"Too bad," said Molly.

"But then we won't look the *same*," said Emily.

All of a sudden, Molly remembered that Emily hadn't had a birthday party in a long time because of the war. No wonder Emily wanted this birthday party to be just so. Molly felt sorry for Emily. "Oh, all right," she said. "We'll wear regular clothes so we'll look like the princesses."

The girls went back to decorating. They put small cups of candy at each place on the table and added noisemakers and blow-out horns. They hung crepe paper streamers across the ceiling. The room began to look ready for a wonderful party. Through the doors to the living room, the girls could hear a radio show beginning. Molly sang along to the music. "My country 'tis of thee . . ." She heard Emily singing softly to the same tune. Emily was singing, "God save our noble king . . ."

"That's an American song," said Molly. "The words are 'My country 'tis of thee.'"

"No, the words are 'God save our noble king,'" said Emily. "It's a British song."

"It is not!" said Molly.

"It is, too!" said Emily. "It's our national anthem!"

"Well, it's an American song now," said Molly.

"It was a British song first," said Emily. "You Americans think everything in the world belongs to you."

"We do not!" said Molly.

"Would you two cut it out?" said Ricky. "I want to listen to this program."

Molly and Emily were quiet. Molly felt as if the heat were turned on too high in the room. She took off her sweater and tossed it on the floor.

"Molly, please," said Mrs. McIntire. "Don't throw your clothes around like that. Can't you take care of your things properly, the way Emily does?"

Molly grabbed her sweater and flung it on a chair. The voice from the radio was the only one in the room. "Battle-weary Britons welcomed more American soldiers today. They call our boys 'the Yanks.' The Yanks bring hope to these tired English people. Everyone knows it's up to these Yanks to save England and the world from Hitler's threat . . ."

"Oh!" said Emily suddenly. "That's not true!"

Everyone was startled. They looked at Emily. Her face was red. "I'm so tired of hearing how America is winning the war when England has been fighting ever so much longer."

"But it's true," said Molly. "England can't win the war without America. Our soldiers are stronger than yours."

"Oh, you Americans!" said Emily. "You always have everything your own way. You think you are so important!"

"We are important," Molly began.

But Mrs. McIntire interrupted. "Girls!" she said. "England and America are allies, remember? We're fighting together." She shook her head at the girls. "I think you are both overtired and overexcited about this party. You two princesses take your imaginary dogs and go upstairs to bed. I'll come up to tuck you in later."

Molly and Emily stalked out of the room, too angry

to look at each other. Molly kept thinking about her party while she got ready for bed. Well, it was supposed to be her party. Now it was "Emily's tea party." Molly threw a candy cup onto the floor.

"Don't!" said Emily. "You'll ruin it."

"Who cares?" said Molly. "Everything is already ruined, and you ruined it. You and your dumb old tea party. I don't want milky tea and lemon tarts! I don't want to wear ugly old clothes!"

"Food and clothes! That's all you ever worry about, nothing important," said Emily. "You don't know anything about what the war is really like. You don't even know what's real. You think the princesses are out of a fairy tale, you pretend you have a dog, and you make a game out of bombing. You're just a spoiled child who has to have everything her own way."

"Spoiled!" said Molly. "I was going to let you share my whole birthday! Now I don't even want you at the party. I let you talk me into doing everything the way you do it in England. In England! I'm so tired of hearing that! If it's so great in England, why don't you just go back there?"

Emily pulled the covers over her head. Molly

thought she heard some sniffles, but she was too mad to care. *I gave in and gave in and gave in to Emily,* she thought. *I'm not giving in anymore. Tomorrow I'll tell Mom we're having a regular American birthday party and Emily's not invited.* And with that thought, Molly pulled the covers over her head and tried to go to sleep.

# Yank and Bennett

sually Molly woke up early and happy on her birthday. But this birthday morning, the dark words she and Emily had said the night before put a shadow on the day. Outside it was gray and cloudy. A cold drizzle was falling. It certainly didn't look like a happy birthday, and Molly didn't feel happy either. She felt bad about the mean things she had said to Emily. She had started by saying she didn't want a lemon tart at the party and ended by saying she didn't want Emily at the party. How did everything get so mixed up?

Molly looked over at Emily's bed. It was empty, perfectly made as usual. Emily was in the bathroom, washing her face. When she came back and saw Molly was awake, she looked away hurriedly. Molly thought Emily looked sorry, too.

Molly tried to think what Dad would do. It was at times like this that she realized how much she needed Dad. Molly looked at Emily's back. One thing was sure: Dad would say that no party was half as important as a friend's feelings. Molly swallowed hard. "Emily . . ." she began.

Emily looked around her shoulder at Molly. At that moment, the door swung open and Mom and Brad burst in. "Happy birthday!" they shouted. "Happy birthday, Molly! Happy birthday, Emily!"

Mom gave both girls a big hug. "Jill! Ricky!" she called. "You can come in now."

Jill and Ricky walked slowly into the room. They were each holding something in their arms. Molly sat up straight in her bed.

"Puppies!" Molly cried. "Puppies! Oh, they're perfect!"

Jill put one puppy on Molly's bed. Ricky put the other puppy into Emily's arms. "We thought you two princesses deserved real puppies," said Mrs. McIntire.

"Yeah, so you can stop acting like nuts, talking to dogs that aren't there," said Ricky.

Everyone laughed and Molly said, "Thank you! A

real puppy! It's too good to be true!" She scooped up her puppy and gave it a kiss. "I love it."

Emily looked at Mrs. McIntire. "Thank you," she said.

Mrs. McIntire smiled. "We'll leave your highnesses to get acquainted with your puppies," she said. "Meanwhile, the rest of us will go make a royal breakfast for you."

Molly's puppy snuggled closer to her chest. It was fat and warm and had snappy brown eyes and pointed ears. Its four little feet were white, as if it had wandered into a puddle of paint by mistake. And it had gingery-red spots, exactly the color of Emily's hair. Molly hugged the puppy. It reached up and licked her under the chin.

"Emily! Emily! Look!" said Molly. "Mine's licking me!"

Emily was cuddling her puppy, too. She rubbed her cheek against its head and murmured. Molly heard her say, "It's been so long."

"What do you mean, 'so long'?" asked Molly.

Emily put her puppy in her lap. She stroked its head. "I used to have a dog," she said. "I didn't tell you before because . . ." Emily paused. "Because my dog was killed. It was one year ago. My dog was trapped under a building that was hit by a bomb."

Molly held her puppy even closer. "Oh, Emily," she said. "That's horrible. I'm so sorry. I'm really, really sorry." Molly brought her puppy over to Emily's bed. The puppies began to play together.

"You know, Emily," Molly went on, "I think you were right about some of the things you said last night. The war has been harder for you. It hasn't been as real for me."

Emily looked at Molly. "I wasn't completely right," she said. "I realized something when I was feeling so bad last night. First I thought about how much I miss my parents. Then I thought, I've only been away from them for a few weeks. Your father has been away from you for two years. I know you miss him very much. The war is hard for you, too, Molly."

Molly nodded. Emily's puppy had the sash of her bathrobe in its mouth. The puppy growled as it tugged and yanked on the sash. Emily and Molly laughed. "Your puppy is a tough little fighter," Molly said. "What are you going to name it?"

"I think I'll call my puppy Yank," said Emily. "Because it's a good American dog."

"I'm going to call my puppy Bennett, after my good English friend," said Molly.

The girls smiled at each other. "Wait till everyone at the party sees our puppies," said Molly. "They'll know we're *really* the princesses." She grinned at Emily. "Even if we don't have crowns and long dresses."

The door opened and Mrs. McIntire stuck her head in. She smiled at the girls, then pretended to scold. "If you princesses weren't such lazybones, lying around in your pajamas all day, you would have found another birthday surprise in your closet by now."

Molly jumped up and opened the closet door. There, side by side, were two white pinafore dresses trimmed with ruffles. The dresses were beautiful. They were absolutely alike. There was one for Molly and one for Emily.

Emily gasped, "They're lovely."

Molly ran over and gave her mother a hug. "Oh, Mom!" she said. "Now everything is perfect. Thank you!"

"Thank you very much *indeed*," said Emily.

Mrs. McIntire said, "You're very welcome, both of you. Now put on your play clothes and come have breakfast. You have a lot to do before your birthday tea party."

Emily picked up her puppy and smiled at Molly. "I think this is a very happy birthday," she said.

Molly smiled back. "Very happy *indeed*."

# Camp Gowonagin

## CHAPTER 6

**T**wo weeks after the birthday tea party, Emily's Aunt Primrose got out of the hospital and Emily went to stay with her. Molly's whole family was sad to see Emily leave. "I'm glad she has Yank to keep her company," Molly had told Mom the day Emily left. The truth was, Molly was glad she had Bennett to keep *her* company. Somehow Molly's room seemed empty without shy, quiet Emily.

Luckily, Emily still came to school, and she and Molly met on the weekends to take their real dogs for real walks on real leashes. The May weather got nicer and nicer, and soon it was June. When school ended, Emily and her aunt took the train to Wisconsin to visit family friends. Molly was disappointed again to see Emily leave, but this time, she was getting ready for her own trip. Molly was going to summer camp!

Molly loved Camp Gowonagin from the very first
day she was there. She and Linda and Susan had never
gone to summer camp before. They were a little nervous when the big old bus that brought them from
home stopped inside the camp's gate. But as soon as
they stepped off the bus with all the other campers,
they were met by cheering Camp Gowonagin counselors. The counselors sang to them:

> Welcome to Camp Gowonagin!
> We're mighty glad you're here!
> Hurray! Hurrah! for Gowonagin!
> Hail! Hail! Let's give a cheer!

"Gosh!" said Susan. "This is neat!"

Molly just grinned happily.

A roly-poly woman came toward them. She was
beaming. "Hello, girls!" she said. "My name is Miss
Butternut. I'm the camp director. Welcome to Camp
Gowonagin! The counselors and I are very happy
you're here."

"Hurray!" cheered the counselors.

Miss Butternut laughed. "You see?" she said to the

campers. "We're going to have a wonderful time. Now, if you'll follow me, I'll show you to your tents."

The campers gathered their suitcases and duffel bags and followed Miss Butternut up the shady path. There were big brown tents on one side of the path. On the other side, Molly saw wide green fields edged with darker green pine trees. The open fields sloped down to a silver-blue lake with an island in the middle. "It's beautiful here," Molly said.

"Yes," said Linda. "There's so much *sky*."

Miss Butternut led Molly, Linda, and Susan to Tent Number Six, where they would live with five other girls. As they carried their gear into the roomy tent, Miss Butternut smiled and said, "Here you are! This is your home sweet home for the next two weeks. Remember our Camp Gowonagin motto, 'Tidy and True.' Keep your tent neat and clean. Then you will be comfortable and happy at Camp Gowonagin."

Molly *was* comfortable and happy at camp right away. The counselors were so nice and friendly, they made everything fun and easy. Molly, Linda, and Susan soon made friends with the girls in their tent and lots of the other campers. "Old campers"—girls who had been at camp last summer—taught them the camp songs and cheers. Molly liked the cheer that went

> Gowonagin! Gowonagin!
> Go on again and try! (Clap, clap)
> You can win! You can win!
> Go on again and try! (Clap, clap)

In just a few days, Molly felt like one of the old campers herself. She knew all the rules and the way everything was done at Camp Gowonagin. She and Linda and Susan kept their tent and their belongings in order. Even Linda, who was messy at home, tried to live up to the "Tidy" part of the camp motto. She always tied her camp tie and kept her shirt tucked in, just like the counselors did.

There was something for everyone at Camp Gowonagin. Linda liked using the bows and arrows in archery. Susan liked campfires, sing alongs, and wienie roasts. Molly liked nature hikes, when Miss Butternut taught them the names of the plants and trees and birds. Every day the girls learned something new and had so much fun that the time just flew by.

Days at camp began early. Miss Butternut stood by the flagpole and blew a cheerful tune on her bugle. The words to the tune were

> I can't get 'em up, I can't get 'em up,
> I can't get 'em up in the morning!

But in Molly's case, the words were wrong. She couldn't wait to get up in the morning and begin the day. There was so much to do! First there was Morning Flag-Raising Ceremony and breakfast in the Dining Hall. Then the campers played games of softball, volleyball, and basketball. They had lessons in swimming, tennis, and sailing. On rainy days, they worked on their arts and crafts projects. Susan was making a leaf and bark chart. Molly was making a sit-upon. She folded a piece of oilcloth around an old newspaper and sewed the edges together. Linda was braiding strings together to make a lanyard—a cord to hang a whistle on and wear around her neck. All the counselors had lanyards. Linda noticed everything about the counselors.

One of Molly's favorite times at camp was Evening Flag-Lowering Ceremony. She liked it because all the girls and all the counselors stood together and sang the Camp Gowonagin song:

> God bless Gowonagin!
> Camp that we love!
> Raise the flag high,
> Never say die,
> While the red, white, and blue flies above!

Molly always got goose bumps up and down her arms when they sang the camp song. Standing shoulder to shoulder with all the other campers made her feel proud. She *did* love Camp Gowonagin. She was glad to be there with her two best friends.

One evening, after the flag was lowered and folded, Miss Butternut said, "Before we go up to dinner, I'm pleased to tell you the winner of the Camp Gowonagin canoe race. First place goes to Dorinda Brassy. Let's have a cheer for Dorinda."

All the campers cheered, "Hip, hip hurray! Hip, hip hurray!"

Dorinda looked smug as everyone cheered. She was an old camper, and she was used to winning.

Miss Butternut went on in her kindly way, "And what do we say to the new camper who came in last?"

All the campers cheered:

> Gowonagin! Gowonagin!
> Go on again and try!
> You can win! You can win!
> Go on again and try!

Miss Butternut nodded happily. "That's the spirit!" she said. "Here at Camp Gowonagin, we know that trying is as important as winning." She smiled. "All right, girls! I'll see you in the Dining Hall in two minutes."

"Go on again and try," repeated Susan as the girls walked up to the Dining Hall. "I *do* try. I just cannot get my canoe to go straight." Susan was the camper who came in last in the canoe race. "No matter what I do, my paddle won't work right," she sighed.

"Well," said Linda glumly, "don't worry. Soon we'll be home, where there's no place to paddle except the bathtub. We have only three more days here." She looked around sadly. "I'm going to miss camp."

"Oh, me too," said Susan. "I'm going to miss absolutely everything at camp except canoeing." She looked at Molly. "You probably feel exactly the way I do, Molly. You're going to miss everything at camp except swimming underwater, right? You hate that the way I hate canoeing."

Molly didn't say anything. She was a little embarrassed. She wished Susan wouldn't compare her poor canoeing with Molly's swimming. "I don't hate swimming," Molly said a little crossly. "I just don't like being underwater. But you don't have to blab it all over the place."

"*I'm* not blabbing it," said Susan. "Everybody in the whole camp knows you won't jump in the water or even get your head wet. We all saw you fall off the dock and almost drown that time."

"Yeah," said Linda. "We saw the counselors save your life. Remember how they jumped right in and pulled you out?"

Molly certainly *did* remember. She would never forget the day she slipped off the dock and fell into the deep water. The dark, dense green water closed over her head. She couldn't see, or breathe, or move.

Though she was only under the water for a few seconds, it seemed like a long, long time to Molly. After the counselors pulled her out, Miss Butternut sat next to her, holding Molly's wet bathing cap, until Molly caught her breath. "Don't you worry," Miss Butternut said. "You'll swim underwater when you're good and ready."

But camp was almost over. And Molly was no closer to swimming underwater than ever.

"Look at it this way," Susan said cheerfully as they sat at their table in the Dining Hall. "You and I will just have to come back to camp next summer, so we can—"

"Go on again and try!" Molly and Linda chimed in. And Molly had to laugh.

Just as they finished dinner, Miss Butternut stood up and said, "Tonight, girls, I have a special announcement to make." She rose up on her toes, as if the good news was trying to spill out by itself. When everyone was quiet, she went on. "One of our favorite traditions here at Camp Gowonagin is our game of Color War."

Whistles and cheers rang out through the Dining Hall. Miss Butternut smiled. "I can see the old campers remember how much fun Color War is! I know the new campers will love it, too. Now, when we play Color War, the whole camp is divided into two teams: the Reds and the Blues. The team lists are on the doors. You may see which team you are on as you leave."

Everyone quickly swung around to look at the doors, as if something as exciting as the lists might shoot off sparks. But the doors looked as quiet as usual.

"Tomorrow morning," said Miss Butternut, "the Red Team will paddle canoes across the narrow part of the lake to Chocolate Drop Island. They'll put the flag at the top of the hill there. It will be the Red Team's job to guard the flag. The Blue Team will have its headquarters here at camp, at the boathouse. They'll try to figure out a way to capture the flag from the Reds. The team that has the flag at sundown wins the game."

Miss Butternut went on. "When the Blues try to capture the flag, they have to be very fast and very smart, or the Red Team will catch them and put them in prison. Prisoners can be freed only if someone from their own team tags them without being caught by the prison guard." Miss Butternut's eyes twinkled. "One last thing," she said. "The counselors and I will be watching you to be sure everyone is safe. But we'll be well hidden, so you probably won't see us." The counselors smiled and nodded. "Any questions?" asked Miss Butternut.

Dorinda Brassy raised her hand. "When will we choose the leaders?" she asked.

"Both teams will meet after dinner to elect their captains," said Miss Butternut. "Anyone may be elected."

"Just look at Dorinda," whispered Linda. "She's *so* sure she's going to be a leader."

Molly looked. Linda was right. Dorinda and her friend Patty already seemed to be taking command. Molly envied them. It would be neat to be in charge. Molly pictured herself leading a team to victory. Her team would capture the flag and canoe back to camp, with everyone cheering and clapping and singing the camp song . . .

"Off you go!" said Miss Butternut.

Molly was practically knocked off her chair by campers charging to see the team lists. By the time Molly got to the doors, she was too far back in the crowd to see anything. But Linda elbowed her way through the crowd to the front, then elbowed her way back to report to Molly and Susan.

"You two are Blues," she said. "I'm a Red."

"Does that mean we're enemies?" asked Susan.

"Not until tomorrow," said Linda with a grin. "I've got to go now. The Red Team is meeting in Tent Number Four to elect a leader. I bet you my bug repellent it'll be Patty. See you later!" She waved as the Reds swarmed out the door.

Later that night, when all the campers were settled in their cots, they heard Miss Butternut play "Taps" on her bugle. That was the signal for lights-out.

Molly listened to the bugle's gentle song. All the girls in the tent sang along softly:

"Day is done.

Gone the sun,

From the lake, from the hills, from the sky.

All is well. Safely rest. God is nigh."

Usually, Molly drifted off to sleep peacefully, wondering what wonderful new activity the next day would bring. But tonight she was too wound up. She turned on her flashlight, rolled over on her side, and whispered to Linda and Susan, "Are you asleep?"

"Nope," said Susan.

"Neither am I," said Linda. "What's the matter?"

"I've been thinking," said Molly. "I'm not sure I like the idea of Color War."

"Me either," said Susan.

"How come?" asked Linda. She flopped over onto her stomach and propped her chin on her pillow.

"Well, in the first place, how do we know what to do?" asked Molly. "I've never been in a Color War before."

"Listen," said Linda. "Isn't little Miss First Place Dorinda the captain of your team? You can bet she will tell you and all the rest of the Blues exactly what to do."

"That's just it," said Molly. "The game sounded like fun when Miss Butternut explained it at dinner. But you should have seen Dorinda at our team's meeting. As soon as she was chosen captain, she started calling us the Blue Army. And she was so serious! She acted like the *general* of a real army."

"Molly's right," Susan agreed. "Dorinda's awfully bossy."

"Yeah," said Molly. "And what if she tells me to do

something terrible, like . . ."

"Like dive in over your head and swim underwater?" Linda finished for her. "If Dorinda tells you to dive, tell her to go jump in the lake. Get it?"

"It's not a joke, Linda," said Molly. "Dorinda's in charge now. I have to do what she says."

"Yes," said Susan. "We're in Dorinda's army now. We have to follow her orders. Everything is different."

"I liked the way camp was before," said Molly. "I don't see why we have to mess everything up and go capturing flags."

"Especially in canoes," added Susan.

Linda shook her head. "It's just a game. It's supposed to be fun, not something to worry about. I mean, if we were going off to a real war or something, then I could see being worried and scared."

Molly nodded. "My dad told us he was scared before he went away to war," she said. "But he said it was okay to be scared because that meant he had a chance to be brave."

"Well, maybe this Color War will give us a chance to be brave," said Linda. "If you can do something you're scared to do, then you're brave."

"That's easy for you to say," said Susan. "You're not scared of canoeing like I am or swimming underwater like Molly is."

"Yeah," said Molly, "you're not scared of anything."

"Oh, yes I am," said Linda.

"Like what?" asked Susan.

"Well," said Linda, "it's really stupid but I'm scared of creepy crawly things, like spiders and bugs. Worms are the worst." Linda moved her fingers like wiggling worms and made a face so that Molly and Susan had to laugh. "Slimy worms! Ugh! I hate them!"

"Really?" said Molly. It cheered her up to know that Linda was scared of something sort of silly, like worms.

"Yes, really," said Linda. "But at least I can joke about it. You don't see me lying awake at night worrying about it. So don't you two worry about Dorinda, or canoes, or swimming underwater. Don't take this Color War so seriously. It won't last forever, right?"

"Right," said Molly and Susan.

"Okay," said Linda. She pulled her blankets up to her chin. "Go to sleep and that's an order!"

"Yes, sir!" giggled Susan. She rolled over and closed her eyes.

Molly turned off her flashlight and closed her eyes, but she didn't follow the order. She didn't fall asleep for a long, long time. Linda wasn't worried about the Color War, but Molly still was. Maybe the Color War would be her big chance to be brave. But she wondered if she really wanted that chance.

# We're in the Army Now

**✪ CHAPTER 7 ✪**

he next morning, every camper put on a red armband or a blue armband to show which team she was on. Right after breakfast, the Red Team left the Dining Hall with the flag. Molly and Susan watched Linda march down the path toward the Red canoes with the rest of her team. They looked like an army, parading two by two like soldiers, carrying their bag lunches, and singing

> We are the Reds,
> Mighty, mighty Reds.
> Everywhere we go-oh,
> People want to know-oh,
> Who we are.
> So we tell them:
> We are the Reds,
> Mighty, mighty Reds . . .

Linda turned around and rolled her eyes at Molly. Molly grinned. She remembered what Linda had said last night about not taking Color War too seriously. *I should be more like Linda,* Molly thought. But she snapped to attention when Dorinda said in her bossiest voice, "Blue Army report to HQ on the double."

"HQ?" Susan asked Molly. "Who's that?"

"It's not a person, it's a place," said Molly. "HQ stands for headquarters. I think she means the boathouse. Let's go."

Molly and Susan followed the rest of the Blue Army to the boathouse. Two girls stood as guards at the door in case the Red Army had left spies behind. When she got the signal that the coast was clear, Dorinda began.

She frowned at the girls. "We are going to win this Color War," she said sternly. "And the only way to win is to fight as hard as we can. Do you understand?"

Everyone mumbled, "Yes."

"All right," Dorinda went on. "Here is the plan of attack. The flag is on Chocolate Drop Island. To get it, we obviously have to canoe across the lake. You will each be assigned a buddy. You and your buddy will paddle a canoe together. We will load up and begin the attack at oh-nine-hundred."

"Oh-nine-hundred?" Susan whispered to Molly. "Where's that?"

"It's not a place, it's a time," said Molly. "It's the army way to say nine o'clock."

"Well, why doesn't she just say nine o'clock?" asked Susan. "We're a team. We're not *really* an army."

Molly put a finger to her lips. Dorinda was scowling at her and at Susan.

"Pay attention, troops!" Dorinda ordered. She turned and uncovered a big map of Camp Gowonagin tacked to the wall.

Everyone said, "Oooh." The map looked as if it had been very carefully drawn. Molly realized Dorinda and her helpers must have been up all night making it. Molly's heart sank. Under Dorinda's command, Color War seemed less and less like a game among friends and more and more like a war between enemies.

The map showed the boathouse, the lake, and Chocolate Drop Island. Dorinda used a long stick to point to places on the map as she talked.

First, she pointed to the boathouse. "We will set out from here," she said. Then she pointed to a place on

the far side of Chocolate Drop Island labeled "Beach."
"We will land here. From the beach we will march up
Chocolate Drop Hill. *I* will capture the flag. The rest of
you will take the Red Army prisoner. You will lead the
prisoners back to your canoes and return them to our
HQ. I will meet you here no later than ten-hundred."

"She means ten o'clock, right?" Susan asked Molly.

But Molly wasn't listening to Susan. There was
something she didn't understand. It wasn't the plan.
She understood the plan perfectly. The plan was easy.
In fact, it was much too easy. Timidly, Molly raised her
hand. Everyone turned around and stared at her.

"Yes?" snapped Dorinda.

Molly stood up. She clasped her hands behind
her back. "Uh, I get the plan," she said. "I know what
we're supposed to do. But I wonder what they're going
to do. The Red Army, I mean. Won't they have scouts
who will see us coming across the lake? The lake isn't
very wide there."

"How do *you* think we should cross the lake?"
Dorinda asked sharply. "Should we swim underwater?"

Molly's hands were clammy. Everyone at camp

knew she hated to swim underwater. She wanted to sit
down, but she made herself speak up. "I just think the
Red Army will be waiting for us at the beach when we
land. They'll be ready to take all of us prisoner. Isn't
there any place we could land where they wouldn't see
us?"

"No," said Dorinda. "Those are my orders."

"But," Molly started to say, "but what if—"

Dorinda crossed her arms over her chest and said,
"If you are too chicken to do this, you can stay behind.
Be a deserter. Otherwise, go with your friend Susan.
The two of you can be buddies and bring up the rear in
your canoe. That way the rest of us can protect you."

Molly sat down, shamed into quiet. She pretended
to straighten her blue armband.

"Now, go to the canoes! The rest of the buddy
assignments will be made there," said Dorinda. Everyone filed out of the boathouse. No one would look at
Molly.

Susan and Molly walked slowly over to the last
canoe on the shore. "How come we don't get lunches
like the Red Army did?" asked Susan. "Won't we get
hungry?"

"We shouldn't need lunches," said Molly. "We're supposed to be back here by ten o'clock, remember?"

"Oh yeah," said Susan. She looked longingly toward the Dining Hall.

"Head out!" they heard Dorinda yell. All the Blues cheered and waved their canoe paddles in the air. Molly pushed the canoe into the water. She started to climb in the back.

"Wait!" said Susan. "I don't want to sit in the front. I'll get splashed by waves up there."

Molly looked at the water. It was as flat as glass. But she said, "Okay, you can sit in the back."

Susan looked uncertain. "Nooo," she said. "I don't want to sit in the back, either. The back person does all the work. You know how bad I am at steering and everything."

"Hurry and make up your mind," said Molly. "The other canoes are already halfway to the island."

"Okay, okay," said Susan. "I'll go in the front. But don't paddle too fast." The canoe wobbled from side to side as Susan climbed in. "See?" she squeaked. "I always get the tippiest canoe." She inched her way to the seat in front, clutching the sides of the canoe with both hands. When she was seated, Molly handed her a paddle, shoved the canoe into deeper water, and climbed in the back. The other canoes were way ahead of them, strung out across the lake like a family of ducks.

As she and Susan paddled closer to the island, Molly could see the Red scout watching them from a high point on the island's shore. The scout turned and ran toward the back side of the island. *She's going to the beach to warn everyone,* Molly thought with a sinking feeling. *The whole and entire Red Army will be waiting for us at the beach. They are going to put us in prison. I just know it.*

The rest of the Blue canoes had already paddled around to the back side of the island, out of Molly's sight. "Come on," she said to Susan. "We'd better catch up with the others." She dug her paddle deep into the water.

Susan dug her paddle in, too. Then she shrieked, "My paddle! I dropped it!"

Molly saw Susan's paddle floating toward her. She put her own paddle in the bottom of the canoe and reached out with both hands to grab Susan's paddle.

Susan was reaching, too, leaning way out over the side of the canoe.

"Don't!" yelled Molly. But it was too late. Over went Susan. Over went the canoe. Over went Molly. Down, down into the water Molly sank, down into the dark green depths. Molly struggled with all her strength, pulling with one arm, grabbing her glasses with the other hand, kicking with her legs, wiggling and fighting her way up. Finally, her head popped out into the sunshine. Molly coughed and choked on the water she had swallowed. She gasped for air.

"Over here!" Molly heard Susan shout. She looked around. Susan was behind her, holding on to the canoe. "Come on!" Susan said. "Grab the canoe!"

Molly swam toward Susan. She held her head up high out of the water. It felt odd, swimming in her clothes. Her shoes felt like weights, dragging her feet down. Molly kicked hard. The canoe was right side up, but it was half full of water. Her paddle floated inside in a big puddle. Molly held on to the canoe and tried to catch her breath.

"I'm so sorry," Susan wailed. "Are you okay? What'll we do?"

"Go to shore," said Molly in a shaky voice. "I think I see a place to land."

They were not far from the island. Both girls held on to the canoe with one arm and pushed through the water with the other arm. As they came to the shore, Molly saw a place where the water cut into the land. She and Susan pushed the canoe into the cut. It was narrow, not much wider than the canoe. They scrambled out of the water and sat on the rocks, panting. Molly was still trembling.

"Gosh," Susan whispered, "I hope the Red Team doesn't catch us."

Molly looked around. They were completely hidden by a high wall of rocky land on one side and tall pine trees on the other. "I don't think anyone can see us here," she said. "The scout is on the other side of those trees, and I think the rest of them are on the far side of the island, on the beach. Probably no one knows about this little place to land. But we'd better not stay long. Let's bail out the canoe."

Molly and Susan scooped water out of the canoe with their Camp Gowonagin hats. When there was still about three inches of water sloshing around the bottom of the canoe, Susan said, "My arms are killing me. Can't we stop now?"

"Okay," said Molly. Her arms hurt, too. "Let's go."

"Good," said Susan. "I'm so hungry. And I want to change my clothes."

"Oh, we can't go back to camp," said Molly firmly. "We have to go on and find the rest of our army."

Susan protested, "But it's nearly lunchtime! And I lost my paddle!"

"I'll paddle," said Molly. She stood up.

Wearily, Susan climbed back into the canoe. "We're probably better off if I don't have a paddle," she said. "We sure can't do any worse."

Molly backed the canoe into the lake by pushing against the rocks with her paddle. Then, slowly, she paddled around the corner of the island until they could see the beach.

"Uh-oh," said Susan.

All the Blue canoes were dragged out of the water on one side of the beach. Paddles stuck out every which way. The canoes looked as helpless as tipped-over turtles waving their legs in the air.

All the girls in the Blue Army were sitting behind

the canoes in a bushy corner of the beach. A big sign on one bush said "PRISON."

"Look at that!" said Susan. "They've got our whole team in their prison, exactly like you said they would."

Standing in front of the prison was a watchful guard with a big whistle on a lanyard around her neck. Molly squinted at the guard through her water-stained glasses. She gasped, "It's Linda! The guard is Linda!" Molly was surprised. She certainly had not expected Linda to have such an important job to do.

"Oh, good," said Susan, relieved. "She can help us." Susan waved her arms above her head. "Yoo-hoo! Linda! It's us!" she shouted. "Help!"

"Susan, I don't know if . . ." Molly began.

At that second, Linda looked straight at Susan and Molly. She put her whistle in her mouth and blew one shrill blast after another. She ran down to the water, swooping toward them like a hawk in attack, waving her arms wildly and pointing to their canoe. Five or six girls with red armbands ran across the beach toward her.

"They'll catch us!" cried Molly. "Let's get out of here!" She paddled hard. Susan stuck her arms in the water and used her hands as paddles. Luckily, the canoe was pretty far out in the lake, and it scooted around to the other side of the island before the Red canoes were even in the water. But Molly didn't stop paddling as hard as she could until she and Susan were all the way across the lake, safe at the boathouse.

Silently, Molly and Susan hauled their canoe out of the water. It was the only canoe on the shore, the last Blue canoe that was free, and it looked lonely. Molly's shoulders were sore. Her hands hurt from gripping the paddle.

Susan shook her head. "I just can't believe Linda would send them out to get us like that," she said. "We're her friends."

"I know," said Molly. "And Linda told us she wasn't going to take Color War too seriously."

"She must have changed her mind," said Susan. "She sure looked serious back there."

"Yeah," said Molly. "She's as serious as Dorinda." Molly felt as if Linda had tricked her in some way. Last night, Linda had said this war would be fun. So far, it had not been very much fun for Molly, that was for sure. *First, I practically drown*, she thought. *Then, even worse, my best friend treats me like an enemy. I guess friend-ship doesn't count during a war.*

Molly and Susan trudged up the hill to their tent. Molly was thinking hard. "After we change clothes, maybe we can dig up some lunch," said Susan. She sounded cheerful.

"First we'd better dig up a plan," said Molly. She sounded serious.

# Creepy Crawlies

hey don't have to be real worms. She just has to think they're worms," said Molly. She and Susan were crawling in the dirt under the wooden platform beneath their tent. They were digging with the cups from their mess kits to find worms. "We can use bugs and spiders, too. I saw lots of them under here last week during Camp Clean-Up. And get sticks and stems like this, see?" Molly held up a stem. It was brown and slimy enough to look like a worm.

"Ugh!" squirmed Susan. "I don't like this plan. I think it's mean."

Molly sighed. "Do you have another idea?" she asked.

"No," said Susan, "but I don't see why we have to do something so mean to Linda. She's our best friend."

"We're not doing it to Linda," said Molly. "We're

doing it to the Red Army. You can't think of people as people during a war. You think of them as part of an army."

"Well . . ." Susan began.

"Look," said Molly sharply. "Linda sure wasn't thinking of us as her friends when she blew the whistle on us, was she?"

"No," admitted Susan.

"So we shouldn't think of her as our friend Linda. We should think of her as the guard for the Red Army. She's got *our* whole army in her prison. We have to get them free or we won't even have a chance to capture the flag and win the Color War. That's why we have to do this," said Molly.

"This" was Molly's plan. It depended on worms. Molly and Susan grubbed in the dirt on their hands and knees. Molly's shirt stuck to her back. Susan's face was red and sweaty.

"I've sweated so much I'm wetter than I was when I fell in the lake," complained Susan.

"Well, we'd better stop," said Molly. Her hands were grimy.

Susan held up an old tin can. It was only half full

of worms and bugs and stems. "There's not very much stuff in here," she said.

"There's not very much *time*," said Molly. "We'll have to go now."

"Okay," said Susan. She and Molly wiggled like worms themselves to get out from under the tent. The sky was white hot as they plodded back to the boat-house.

Molly pushed the canoe into the water. She started to get in the back.

Susan said, "No sir! I'm not getting in the front again. That's the tippiest part."

"No it isn't," said Molly.

But Susan was stubborn. "I'm NOT getting in the front of that canoe again, and that's final. Do you want to tip over like the last time?"

Molly remembered her plunge into the water. "All right," she said. "I'll get in the front. But I won't be able to help you paddle. The Red scout has got to think there's only one of us in the canoe or she might guess the plan."

"Well, you lie down," said Susan. "The scout won't be able to see you."

So Molly lay down on the bottom of the canoe next to the extra paddle, and Susan pushed off. With Susan paddling, the canoe jerked forward like a darting fish. It rolled from side to side, but it did move. Soon Susan said, "There's the Red scout. She sees me."

"Just keep paddling," hissed Molly. They were not far from the island. The canoe zigzagged, sometimes heading away from the island, then heading straight for it.

"Susan," said Molly, "you're supposed to switch your paddle from side to side every few strokes so the canoe will go in a line."

"I can't do it that way," said Susan shortly. "I'm doing it the only way I know how."

"Maybe that's good," said Molly. "It will confuse the Red scout. She won't be able to figure out what you're trying to do. Now, head for that hidden landing place we found last time."

In a surprisingly short time, they got to the landing place they'd found when the canoe tipped over. Susan banged the canoe on the rocks, but she managed to get it into the narrow space.

Molly sat up. "Okay," she said. "Give me your

paddle. Here are the worms." The plan was for Molly to paddle the canoe around to the beach. Susan would climb around the edge of the island to the prison and free the rest of the Blue Army. Then she would swim out to Molly and the canoe.

But Susan held on to the paddle. "Listen," she said, "the Red scout just saw me paddling across the lake. Won't she think it's funny if she sees you paddle around to the beach? I think I should stay with the canoe and you should do the worm and prisoner part."

"But that means you'll have to handle the canoe all by yourself," said Molly. "Are you sure you can do it?"

Susan shrugged. "I don't know," she said. "I got us this far, maybe I can do the rest. Anyway, I'll try."

"You're pretty brave," Molly said.

"You've got the hard part," said Susan. "You might get caught by the Red Army."

"No," said Molly with a little grin. "I figure they will be so busy watching the way you paddle a canoe, they'll never notice me."

Susan smiled. "Good luck," she said. As Molly scrambled up the rocks, Susan backed the canoe into the lake.

Molly moved as quickly as she could, staying very close to the water. For a while she could see Susan's canoe moving along offshore. Then the canoe disappeared around a point of land and Molly couldn't see it anymore.

Molly crept around the shore toward the prison. She kept a sharp lookout for the Red Army. Suddenly, Molly stopped. Here was a surprise. The path was gone! She was standing at the edge of an inlet that cut into the shore of Chocolate Drop Island. Molly could see the prison on the other side of the inlet. *Why wasn't this inlet on Dorinda's map?* Molly asked herself. The water looked deep. *Well,* thought Molly, *I'll just have to swim across to get to the prison. There's no other way.*

She put the can of worms down her undershirt and tucked her shirt tightly into her shorts. Then she waded into the water. When it reached her shoulders, Molly dog-paddled as quietly as she could, keeping her head well above the water. When she was about halfway across, she stopped. *Oh, no!* she thought. *Linda!* Linda was walking through the bushes behind the prison. She was coming right toward Molly. Linda's whistle glinted in the sun.

Molly held her breath, as if that would make her invisible. *If Linda sees me, I'm done for,* she thought. *The whole Blue Army is done for!* But there was no place to hide in the middle of the water. There was nowhere to go but . . .

*Down,* thought Molly. *I'll have to swim underwater.* Molly shuddered. *I just can't make myself do it,* she thought. But Linda was coming closer and closer and closer . . . Quickly, Molly took a deep breath and slid down under the surface.

The water swallowed her. She forced herself to open her eyes. Greeny gold sunlight filtered through the water. Plants writhed like snakes next to her. *Maybe if I move it won't be so bad,* Molly thought. She fluttered her legs and pulled with her arms. The can of worms was cold against her skin.

Finally, she couldn't hold her breath any longer. She bobbed up for air. Thank goodness! Linda had turned her back. She was moving away from Molly, watching something out in the big lake off the opposite end of the beach. It was Susan, waving her paddle around, slapping it against the water, calling, "Yoo-hoo! Yoo-hoo!"

The Red Army girls were all watching Susan. They buzzed like confused bees. "Get the canoes! We've got to take her prisoner!" one girl yelled. "No, she's coming to shore," yelled another. Susan kept them guessing. She zigged toward the land one second, then zagged out into deeper water the next second. But all the while, she was leading the girls farther and farther down the beach, far away from the prison. Only Linda stayed near it, standing guard.

Molly scuttled out of the inlet like a crab, keeping an eye on Linda the whole time. She hid behind a bush while she caught her breath. But there was no time to waste. She pulled the lid off the can and sneaked quietly toward the prison. When Linda's back was turned, Molly dashed up behind her and yelled, "WORMS!" She dumped the stuff in the can on Linda's head. Spiders and stems went down the back of Linda's shirt. Sticks and bugs fell over her face. Worms were caught in her hair.

"ARRGH!" Linda howled. "Help!" She clawed at her hair, trying to pull the worms off. She jumped up and down wildly. Then she turned and saw Molly. "You?" she cried.

Molly froze. She was supposed to tag Linda and take her prisoner. She couldn't do it. This was Linda, her friend. She didn't look like the fierce Red Army guard anymore. She was plain old Linda, and she looked like she was going to cry.

Molly ran away. She rushed toward her teammates who were prisoners. "Blue Army! Blue Army! You're free!" she yelled as she tagged them. "Follow me! Hurry up!"

With a great cheer, the Blue Army stampeded out of the prison. Linda didn't stop anyone. She was still pulling worms out of her hair. The Blue Army girls dragged their canoes into the lake, jumped into them, and paddled furiously, churning the water white. Some girls swam next to the canoes as their buddies paddled, and others had a leg up on the side of their canoes, trying to climb aboard.

When the Red Army girls saw what was happening, they ran crazily in all directions. Some headed up the hill to protect the flag. Some ran across the beach toward the prison. Some went to their canoes to try to chase the Blue Army. They were shouting, stumbling, and bumping into each other.

Susan paddled her canoe toward Molly, coming close to the shore. Molly swam as fast as she could to the canoe. "Get in! Get in!" cried Susan.

Molly pulled herself into the canoe. Carefully, Susan leaned way to the other side to balance Molly's weight. When she was safe in the canoe, Molly turned back to look at the beach.

Linda was standing all alone. Her hands hung down at her sides. She wasn't even trying to blow her whistle.

Molly made herself turn away. She picked up her paddle and followed the rest of the Blue Army back to camp. The war wasn't over yet, but Molly felt as if she had already lost something very important.

# Victory at Sea

 he Blue Army was rather quiet by the time everyone got back to the boathouse. "Here we are," sighed one girl. "Right back where we started."

Molly looked at the downhearted girls. No one knew what to do. "Where's Dorinda?" Molly asked.

A girl named Marie spoke up. "Dorinda wasn't in the same prison with the rest of us. She was in a special captain's prison. She didn't see you. I guess she's still on the island."

"Serves her right," someone muttered.

"What'll we do now?" a tall girl named Shirley asked. "Should we give up?"

"No!" said Molly. "We can win the war without Dorinda."

"But who will be our leader?" asked Marie.

"I think it should be Molly," said Susan loyally. "She thought up the plan to free all of you. I didn't like it, but it worked. She can think up another plan to capture the flag and win the whole Color War. Can't you, Molly?"

"Yes," said Marie. "You be our captain, Molly."

Molly felt a little tickle of pride. But quickly, she felt something else, too. *What if our army is captured again? Everyone will blame me. I will be the one who lost the war,* she thought. *I wonder if this is the way real leaders feel. I bet they felt this way before the D-Day invasion.* Molly thought about the newsreels she had seen of the D-Day invasion. The soldiers spilled out of the boats, ran across the beach, scrambled up the rocky cliffs along the shore . . .

"Well?" Susan was asking her. "Do you have a plan?"

"I was just thinking," said Molly slowly. "Our Color War is sort of like the real war. We have to do what the Allies did on D-Day." Molly began to talk faster as she got excited. "The enemy—the Red Army—knows we're going to try to land and invade their territory, just like the Nazis knew the Allies were going to land and invade France. The only thing they didn't know was exactly when and exactly where the Allies would land."

"Oh, for heaven's sake," said Shirley. "In our war, the *when* is this afternoon and the *where* is the beach. There's no other time or place."

"We can't land on the beach again," said Molly, thinking out loud. "That's the mistake we made last time. The Red Army will be waiting for us there. We have to land someplace where they don't expect us."

"Like where?" Shirley asked.

Molly had an idea. She stepped over the sitting girls and went to the map. "Susan and I found a place when we fell out of—I mean, when we went to the island before," she said. "It's right . . . here!" Molly pointed to the map. She put her finger on the narrow landing place on Chocolate Drop Island. "It's a good place to land because the Red scout can't see it. It's hidden by rocky land on one side and trees on the other." Molly read the name off the map. "It's called Poison Point."

"But Molly," Susan piped up, "it's an awfully skinny place. Only one canoe can fit in it at a time."

"That's no good then," said Shirley. "We can't

unload one canoe, then back it out, then unload the next. It would take too long. And how would we keep the empty canoes from floating away? We need a long beach or a long dock."

"Maybe we could build a dock on the island," said Marie.

"That's silly," said Shirley.

"No it isn't," said Molly. She thought of the D-Day newsreels again. "We can build a floating dock. That's what the Allies did when they landed in France."

Everyone looked blank.

"Don't you remember the newsreels we saw of D-Day?" Molly asked. "The Allies built a long, long dock from the deep water all the way to the shore. Remember? They built it out of barges and boats. They could drive trucks off their big ships and onto their dock, and then all the way to land."

"I don't get it," said Susan. "We don't have any barges or anything. What can we use to build a dock?"

"Canoes," said Molly. "We'll use our canoes. We'll land one canoe at Poison Point, then we'll tie another canoe to it. We'll tie all the canoes to one another, end to end, in a long row. We can use our Camp

Gowonagin ties. Then we'll walk from canoe to canoe, onto the island."

The girls murmured among themselves. "That's crazy," someone said.

"Yes, but it might work," said Molly.

"I think we should try it," said Marie.

"All right, then!" Molly said. "Let's go!"

Susan was taking one last look at the map. "How come that place is called Poison Point?" she asked. "Are the rocks poison or something?"

But no one was there to answer Susan's question. Everyone was climbing back into the canoes. "Okay," shouted Molly. "I'll give each canoe a number. That will be your place in line. Susan will be in the first canoe and I will be in the last one." Molly pointed to each canoe. "One! Two! Three! Four! Five! Six! Seven! Eight! Nine! Ten! Ready? Head out!"

The Blue Army canoes followed Susan's canoe across the lake. Molly noticed Susan seemed to be paddling much straighter. Her canoe didn't zig and zag as much as it used to. When they got close to the island, Molly saw the Red scout watching them. The scout turned and ran back toward the beach.

*Good,* thought Molly. *They think we're silly enough to land on the beach again. The Red Army will be there waiting for us. They won't expect us to sneak up on them from behind.*

Susan slipped her canoe into the landing place at Poison Point. Canoe Number Two pulled up behind her canoe, and Susan tied them together. In no time, all ten canoes were tied end to end. The girls kept low as they crawled from canoe to canoe onto the island. Canoe Number Four almost turned over, but luckily no one was in it at the time. Molly was the last one to cross the rickety canoe dock onto the land.

"Okay!" she said to the girls gathered on the point. "Everyone from the first five canoes, go around to the beach. You'll have to swim a little, because there's an inlet just before you get to the prison. But you'll be able to sneak up on the Reds from behind the prison. Bring your Red Army prisoners back to camp in their own canoes. Everyone else will come up the hill with me to capture the flag. Let's go!"

No one moved.

"What's the matter?" asked Molly, exasperated.

"We found out why it's called Poison Point," said

Susan. "This whole place is covered with poison ivy. No one wants to crawl through it."

Molly was determined. "We can't quit now," she said. "We have to . . . we have to . . .

Gowonagin! Gowonagin!

Go on again and try!"

The girls looked at each other uncomfortably.

Molly marched up and sat down smack in the middle of the poison ivy. She said,

"You can win! You can win!

Go on again and try!"

The girls giggled. Then Susan climbed up toward Molly. One by one every girl in the Blue Army followed her. The girls climbed over the rocks carefully, trying to avoid the poison ivy leaves. One group headed toward the beach. The other group followed Molly up Chocolate Drop Hill.

At the top of the hill, Molly saw six Red Army girls guarding the flag. They were sitting in the sun eating their lunches, so they did not see Molly and the Blue Army sneaking up on them.

"One, two, three!" whispered Molly. She and her group fanned out, two Blue Army girls tagging each of the Red guards. Molly rushed to the very top of the hill. She pulled the flag out of the ground and waved it over her head.

"HURRAY!" the Blue Army girls cheered, jumping up and down and hugging one another. The Red guards were too stunned to do anything. Molly led everyone in a happy race back down the hill to the canoes. No one seemed to worry about poison ivy on the way down.

As Molly's group got back to Poison Point, the rest of the Blue Army came paddling around the island in the Red canoes they'd captured. In each canoe there was one Blue Army girl and two Red Army prisoners. When the Blue Army girls saw Molly and the flag, they cheered, "Yahoo! We win! Hurray, Blue Army! Hurray, Molly! Hurray! Hurray!"

Molly looked for Linda, but she couldn't find her in the crowd. She did see Dorinda, who was the only Blue Army girl who was not cheering. Molly sat in the middle of a canoe, holding the flag above her head. Across the lake they went. The canoes followed a glittering path made by the late afternoon sun. Molly listened to the girls singing:

Raise the flag high,
Never say die,
While the red, white, and blue flies above!

Their voices were full of happiness. Molly was happy, too. The Color War was over.

# The Pink Army

iss Butternut and the counselors were waiting at the boathouse when the girls got back to camp. Molly was very glad to see the camp director's round, cheerful face. She felt relieved when she put the flag in Miss Butternut's hands.

Miss Butternut looked a little confused. "Uh, congratulations, Blues," she said. "Good job, Captain . . . Molly."

"Oh, I'm not the captain," said Molly. "Dorinda is really in charge."

"I see," said Miss Butternut. She looked over at Dorinda, who was sulking. "Well," Miss Butternut said briskly, "you can tell us the whole exciting story later. But right now, I think everyone on both teams should report to the Dining Hall for a celebration. Ice cream cones for everyone!"

"Hurray! Ice cream!" shouted the girls. They ran up the hill to the Dining Hall.

As Molly was scooping ice cream into her cone, Miss Butternut said, "The counselors and I saw most of what happened, but we don't know *why* it happened that way. Perhaps you can tell us how it is that *you* ended up capturing the flag, Molly."

Molly didn't know where to begin. "Well . . ." she started.

Susan hurried forward. "*I'll* tell," she said. "Molly really saved the day. She did everything. You see, Dorinda was in prison. Actually, everybody in the Blue Army was in prison except Molly and me, because I tipped over our canoe. Then Molly thought up a plan to throw worms on Linda, because she was the prison guard, so we could free the Blue Army. We freed everybody, all except Dorinda. Then nobody knew what to do. So Molly thought up another plan. This time, we paddled over to Poison Point—"

"To where?" Miss Butternut interrupted. She sounded worried.

"To Poison Point," Susan said. "We climbed—"

"WAIT!" cried Miss Butternut. She jumped up and

stood on a chair. She blew a blast on her bugle and waved her other arm wildly. Everyone was so surprised, they were absolutely still. The Dining Hall had never been so quiet.

"Girls! Girls!" said Miss Butternut. "Stop! Before you get your cones, everyone who was at Poison Point go to the showers immediately. I want you to scrub, and I mean *scrub*, with strong soap. Then report to the camp nurse for calamine lotion." Miss Butternut shook her head. "I'm afraid it's already too late. The whole bunch of you is going to have a walloping case of poison ivy!"

All the girls groaned.

Miss Butternut hurried the girls out of the Dining Hall. Even her hair looked frazzled. Her gray curls were standing out from her head like ruffled feathers.

Molly and Susan joined the sad parade. "Some victory celebration," sighed Susan. "Only the losers go to the party. The winners have to go to the nurse." Discouraged, Molly and Susan plodded up the path to their tent to get their towels.

"Hey!" someone shouted. They turned around. It was Linda. "Wait up!" she said.

When Linda caught up to them, she was panting. "Here," she said. She gave each of them an ice cream cone.

"Gee, thanks!" said Susan. She was much cheerier. "It's nice of you to bring us ice cream. We thought you were mad at us about the worms."

Molly looked at Linda out of the corner of her eye.

"Well . . ." said Linda, a little sheepishly, "I was mad. But then I figured you were mad at me for blowing the whistle on you."

"We were surprised," said Molly. "We didn't expect you to be so serious about the game."

Linda shrugged. "I guess I kind of wanted the counselors to be proud of me," she said.

"Oh," said Molly.

"Well, if you ask me, it was a very mixed-up day. No one acted normal," said Susan. She had a dab of ice cream on her nose. "You were so serious we had to throw worms at you. I spent the whole day in a canoe. And Molly swam underwater, even though no one asked her to."

Linda turned to Molly. "No kidding?" she asked. "You swam underwater?"

"Yes," said Molly, "I did."

"Gosh," said Linda. "Then you *do* deserve to win the Color War."

Molly grinned. "I don't think anybody really won this war. I'm just glad it's over."

"Me, too," said Linda.

"Me, too," said Susan. "Now we can all have fun together, like before."

"Yes," said Molly. "I don't want to be a Red or a Blue or any other color ever again!"

But by the next morning, Molly, Susan, and almost everyone else at Camp Gowonagin *was* another color: POISON IVY PINK! The girls had bumpy red rashes on their arms, legs, and faces. They were all covered in pink calamine lotion, which helped soothe their itchy skin. Despite being sore and scratchy, Molly was happy. She and Linda and Susan were all on the same team again, and they were going to make the most of their last day at camp. As they headed to the Morning Flag-Raising Ceremony, Molly knew she would come back to Camp Gowonagin next year . . . but that she would stay far, far away from Poison Point.

# Hurray for the U.S.A.!

olly and her friends returned to Jefferson, and all too soon, school started again. Molly was happy that she and Linda and Susan were all in the same fourth-grade class. But Molly wasn't happy when another Christmas came and went without her father. A new year—1945—began, and she wondered how much longer her family would have to wait to see Dad again. Molly was trying to be patriotically patient, but it wasn't easy.

On a cold, rainy afternoon in March, Molly, Linda, and Susan stood at the bus stop waiting for the city bus to come and take them home. They had to wait under the movie theater sign to stay dry. But the girls didn't even notice the rain or the cold. They were too excited. They'd just come from their tap dance lesson at Miss LaVonda's, so they were warm and sweaty.

"Our show is going to be the best show anyone ever saw," said Molly happily.

"I can't wait!" said Susan. "I've never been in a big show like this before."

"Well, there's never *been* a show like this in Jefferson before," said Linda. "Practically everyone in the whole town has a part in it, singing or dancing or playing in the band."

"Even my mom is in the show," said Molly. "She's going to make a speech about the Red Cross Blood Drive."

"Our part is the best part of all," Susan gloated. "Miss LaVonda said so. She said we're the grand finally."

"The grand finn—*al*—lee," corrected Linda.

"Oh, whatever," said Susan cheerily. "We're the flag. And the flag is the most important thing in the show."

Miss LaVonda, the girls' tap dance teacher, was in charge of a big show called "Hurray for the U.S.A." The show was being put on at the Veterans' Hospital in Jefferson. The hospital was full of soldiers who had been hurt or wounded in the war.

Molly, Linda, Susan, and the rest of the girls in their tap dance class were the last act in the show. They were going to dance and sing a patriotic song. They would wear red, white, and blue costumes so that together they formed a giant flag on the stage. At one point in the song, the flag would part in the middle and one girl would do a special tap dance all by herself. She was Miss Victory, and her solo was a real showstopper.

Miss LaVonda had not picked a girl to be Miss Victory yet. While the girls were rehearsing, she danced that part herself. But during the next week, every girl in the class was going to have a chance to try out to be Miss Victory. Molly already knew the special solo dance by heart.

"I can do that Miss Victory dance in my sleep," she said to Linda and Susan. She closed her eyes, held her umbrella up high, and did the complicated dance steps right there on the sidewalk. Linda and Susan sang the music for her. "Ta-da!" she said at the end.

"Gosh!" exclaimed Susan as the girls climbed on the bus. "That was great, Molly. You can make that dance look good even in your galoshes! I'm sure you'll get to be Miss Victory."

"Well," said Molly generously, "everyone gets to try out. Either of you could be Miss Victory, too."

"Nope. Not me," said Linda. She plopped down in the seat in front of Molly and Susan. "I'd be too nervous all alone out there in front of everybody. I'd forget all the hard steps and just stand there like a dope. I don't want to be Miss Victory."

"Me either," said Susan. "You'll be Miss Victory for sure, Molly. Everybody says so."

Molly blushed. She was very pleased. "I sure would like to be Miss Victory," she said. She tapped the dance steps on the floor of the bus even though she was sitting down. "I love the costume."

"Oh, it's gorgeous," agreed Susan.

Miss Victory's costume was made of shiny blue and red satin and sparkly silver material. There was a big silver star on one shoulder, and a star crown for Miss Victory to wear on her head.

Linda turned sideways to look back at Molly. "You *should* be Miss Victory," she said loyally. "You dance the best, so that would be fair. But sometimes these things aren't exactly fair."

"Miss LaVonda is fair," Susan said. "She wants the

best dancer to be Miss Victory, and that's Molly."

"I know, I know," said Linda. She squirmed a little. "But, well, in a show, a lot depends on how a person looks, not just how she sings or dances. I mean, think about that silver star thing Miss Victory is supposed to wear on her head. It will only look right on somebody with curly hair. It would look dumb on somebody with straight hair like mine—"

"Or braids like mine," interrupted Molly glumly. All her high hopes of being Miss Victory had fallen with a thud. She knew Linda was right, as usual.

Linda nodded sadly at Molly. "Yeah, I'm afraid braids would look dumb, too," she said. "No offense, Molly."

"Molly has very . . . *normal* hair," said Susan. "Miss LaVonda won't care."

"No, Linda is right," said Molly. "Miss Victory should have beautiful curls. My hair is just brown sticks." She pulled her slicker hat down over her ears and looked out the window at the weepy rain.

"Well, there's no point in getting upset about it," said Linda kindly. "Let's face it. Your hair is just plain straight. It comes out of your head that way. You can't do anything about it."

"Oh yes you can," said Susan. "My sister Gloria's hair is really sort of clumpy, but she gave herself a home permanent wave, and now she has lots of curls."

Molly was interested. "Gloria gave herself a permanent?" she asked.

"Yeah, sure! It was easy," said Susan breezily. "You just get a box of permanent lotion and you wash your hair—or maybe you don't wash your hair, I forget. Anyway, you put the lotion on and set your hair on these special sort of curlers, and then it dries and you take the curlers out and you have beautiful curls."

Linda looked doubtful. "I don't know," she said. "My aunt gave herself one of those home permanents, and she ended up looking like a French poodle."

"It doesn't matter anyway," said Molly. "My mother would never let me have a permanent wave."

"Well, she wouldn't need to know until afterward," Susan pointed out. "And by that time you'd already have the curls."

Molly thought about that as the girls got off the bus at their stop. "Does the home permanent kit cost a lot?"

"I don't think so," said Susan. "You could use your

Saturday movie money."

"That wouldn't be enough," said Linda.

"Then I'll chip in *my* movie money," Susan said firmly. "Molly needs to get curls."

Linda looked at Molly. "Do you really want a permanent?"

"Well, I really want to be Miss Victory," Molly answered slowly. "And it does seem like a permanent might help. So . . ."

"Okay," said Linda. "I'll chip in my movie money, too. But I'm still not sure about this permanent wave business. It seems risky to me."

"Oh, don't worry, Linda," said Susan. "I know all about it. I'll give Molly the permanent. It will look gorgeous. You'll see."

When Molly got home, Brad was sitting at the kitchen table coloring, and Mom was helping Ricky with his homework.

"Hello, dear," said Mrs. McIntire. "Leave your galoshes on the newspaper by the door, please. Mrs. Gilford washed the floor today. How was tap dancing?"

"Fine," said Molly. She was thinking so hard about getting a permanent that she was frowning.

Mrs. McIntire looked up. "Why so glum, chum? You're usually so happy after dancing class."

"She must have caught sight of herself in a mirror," said Ricky. "Yikes! That would make *anyone* glum."

"Har dee har har," said Molly. "That's so funny I forgot to laugh."

"Well, I have something that will cheer us all up," said Mom. "It's a letter from Dad. I've been waiting for everyone to be home before I read it. Ricky, call Jill. Let's all go into the living room."

When everyone was settled, Mom began. "Dear Merry McIntires . . ." Suddenly, she stopped. "Oh!" she exclaimed.

"What? What is it?" everyone asked.

Mrs. McIntire's face was glowing. She tried hard to keep her voice calm, but it was so full of happiness it sounded wobbly. She read, "I'm coming home . . ." and everyone exploded.

"HURRAY! YIPPEEE! DAD! DAD! DAD!"

Molly danced around the room with Jill. Ricky cheered, "Yahoo! Hurray!" Brad hugged his mother, who was wiping tears from her eyes.

"Settle down now!" said Mrs. McIntire, laughing.

"Do you want to hear the rest?"

Everyone got quiet and listened as she read

> *My orders have been changed. I'm coming*
> *back to the states to take care of the wounded*
> *soldiers at the Veterans' Hospital in Jefferson.*
> *I'll be able to live at home! No one can tell*
> *me for sure exactly when I'll get home. But it*
> *looks like I might be there by the eighteenth of*
> *March. Maybe in time for lunch.*
>
> *It will be so wonderful to see all of you! I*
> *can tell by the pictures you sent that Ricky is*
> *probably a basketball star by now, and Brad*
> *isn't a baby anymore. And Jill! You look so*
> *grown-up and sophisticated in your prom*
> *dress! You've become a beauty just like your*
> *mother. And of course, I can't wait to see*
> *good old olly Molly and taste Mrs. Gilford's*
> *perfect pot roast. I'll be so glad to get home!*
> *Hurray for the U.S.A.!*
>
> *Lots of love,*
> *Dad*

"Well!" exclaimed Mrs. McIntire as everyone cheered again. "Well! I can hardly believe it! This is the news we've been waiting for ever since Dad left!"

"And March eighteenth is only two weeks from now," said Jill.

"Oh, it will be so great to have him home again!" said Molly.

"How will Dad get here?" asked Brad.

"I'm not sure," said Mrs. McIntire. "I guess he'll come on the train."

"I think we'd better pick him up at the station," said Brad. "He might not remember where our house is."

"Don't worry, dear," said Mrs. McIntire. "I'm sure Dad will find us."

"Let's phone Gram and Granpa and tell them the good news!" said Jill.

"Good idea!" said Mrs. McIntire. She started to put the letter back in the envelope.

"Oh, may I see the letter?" asked Molly. She wanted to read it by herself. It was such wonderful news! Dad was coming home!

She read along and came to the last paragraph,

where Dad said Ricky was a basketball star, Brad
had grown up, Jill was a sophisticated beauty, and
Molly . . . Molly was just good old olly Molly, men-
tioned in the same sentence as pot roast.

Molly felt disappointed and a little hurt. Dad
sounded so pleased and proud of the way everyone
else had changed. But he didn't say anything about
how *she* had changed at all. Did he think she was just
the same dumb little kid she'd been when he left? She
would have to show him that she had grown up, that
she was different now, so that he would be proud of
*her*, too. But how could she do it?

Molly began to have a wonderful idea. The show!
The "Hurray for the U.S.A." show! Dad would be
home in time to see it. What if Dad saw her on the
stage, in front of a huge audience, dancing the special
Miss Victory solo dance, looking beautiful in the sparkly costume, wearing the silver crown on top of long,
lovely curls? *Then* he would see she was grown-up and
different! He'd be so surprised and proud!

Right then Molly made up her mind. She would get
a permanent wave so that she would have curls. She
would be Miss Victory. And Dad would see her in the

show, looking beautiful.

Everything would be perfect.

# A Hair-Raising Experience

hat night, Molly couldn't sleep. *Dad's coming home, Dad's coming home,* she kept thinking.

She felt the excitement growing, growing, growing inside until she thought she'd burst with happiness.

She kept imagining how it would be when Dad saw her in the show. She would be wearing the glamorous Miss Victory costume. All the lights would be shining on her. Silver stars would sparkle in her curly hair. Dad would watch her do the complicated tap dance. Afterward, backstage, Dad would say, "Why, Molly! You've changed so much. You're so grown-up and sophisticated! Just as much as Jill!" Then they'd all come home and celebrate. Molly went through the wonderful imaginary scene again and again.

Molly rolled over and stared up at the ceiling.

What would it be like to have Dad home again after he'd been away at war for two years? What would it be like to have him back in the house? Molly could remember the warm, vanilla-y smell of his pipe tobacco and the sound of his voice calling out, "I'm home!" at the end of the day. But Dad's face was a little blurry in her memory. She scrunched up her eyes and tried to picture Dad's face clearly—the way he really looked, not the way he looked in his army uniform in the shadowy black-and-white snapshots he sent from England. She couldn't seem to see him.

Finally, Molly got out of bed and tiptoed downstairs to the living room to look at the old photo albums. She sat cross-legged on the couch, holding the biggest album on her lap. She stared and stared at the pictures pasted to the black pages. There was a funny one of Dad painting the garage. He looked so tall and handsome and happy. On the next page, there was a picture of the whole family together, taken at Thanksgiving a few months before Dad left for the war. It was very discouraging. *Everyone but me looks so different now,* thought Molly. *I look exactly the same now as I did then. Just plain old me.*

"Molly!" she heard Mom say. "I *thought* I saw a light down here. Why are you up?"

"I couldn't sleep," said Molly. "I keep thinking about Dad coming home."

"Me, too," said Mom. She sat next to Molly on the couch.

"It's so wonderful that he'll be home on the eighteenth of March," said Molly. "He can see all of us in the show."

"Now, Molly," said Mom. "Don't go getting your hopes up. Dad said he *might* be here on the eighteenth. But the army often changes plans at the last minute. I'm sure Dad will do his best to get here in time for the show, but you can't count on it."

Molly knew Mom was being sensible, but she was still sure Dad would be home in time to see her as Miss Victory. It would just be so perfect! She didn't want to hear any discouraging warnings, so she said, "I sort of couldn't remember what Dad looked like. That's why I got out the old albums."

Mom held half the album on her lap. She looked at the Thanksgiving picture. "Granpa took this picture. I remember that day very well," she said. "There I am in my polka-dot dress. It was new back then. I still wear that dress sometimes. It doesn't look so stylish anymore." She sighed, "Neither do I, I'm afraid." She pushed a lock of hair behind one ear. "Look at Brad! He was just a baby. He looks so different now."

"Do you think Dad will look different?" asked Molly.

"He probably will," said Mom. "He'll probably look a little thinner and a little older, just as I do."

"Do you think he'll act different?" Molly asked.

"I don't know," said Mom. "He has seen some very sad and terrible things during the war. War does change people. It doesn't just happen and then disappear, all forgiven and forgotten. War leaves scars on people, and not just the kind of scars you can see. But I think Dad will still be our same old Dad at heart. He'll still love us. We'll all have to get used to one another again. It may take some time. We're all older. We're all different."

"I sure want Dad to see that I'm different," said Molly. "I want him to see that I'm grown-up now, not just a plain dumb kid anymore. But the problem is, I don't *look* different."

Mom hugged Molly. "Your dad will be so happy to see you, he won't care what you look like," she said. "You know he'll always love you and be proud of you, no matter what."

"Mothers always say that," said Molly.

"Because it's true!" said Mrs. McIntire with a smile. "And here's another thing mothers always say: Get to bed! Tomorrow is a school day. Besides, it's cold down here. You don't want to greet Dad with a red nose and sniffles, do you? Come on, now. Off to bed. Lickety-split!"

"Okay," said Molly. She hugged her mother and went back upstairs, carrying the photo album with her. *I WILL look different, though,* she said to herself. *I can't wait to get that permanent.*

However, Molly did have to wait. She had to wait two more days, until Saturday, when she and Linda and Susan got their movie money. The movie cost twenty-five cents, and they all got nickels for popcorn. Susan's mother always gave her an extra nickel in case of emergency. Luckily, Molly had thirty cents left over from a dollar Granpa had given her for Christmas, so they had just enough money. The permanent wave kit cost $1.25.

"It's really nice of you to give up your movie money," Molly said to Linda and Susan as the girls headed to the drugstore.

"Well," said Linda, "I hear this movie has lots of kissing and mushy stuff in it, so I don't care about missing it." Linda liked Westerns.

"*Besides*," said Susan, "your dad is coming home. This is going to be the most important moment of your whole and entire life so far! You've got to have those curls. Not just to be Miss Victory, but to show your dad how grown-up and sophisticated you are. It's so exciting!"

Molly nodded. "I can't believe he's finally coming home, after all this time," she said.

"You're so lucky, Molly," said Susan. "Your father's coming home safe and sound."

"Yeah, not like Grace Littlefield's father," said Linda. Mr. Littlefield's legs had been wounded in the war, and he would never walk again.

"Poor Grace," said Molly softly.

"It would be terrible to have a father who couldn't

walk anymore," said Susan.

"I bet Grace is just happy he's home and alive," said Linda. "Think about Miss Campbell."

All the girls got quiet. Their third-grade teacher, Miss Campbell, had been engaged to marry a soldier who was killed during the summer.

"I wonder if Miss Campbell's soldier ever thought he might be killed and be dead forever and never get to marry Miss Campbell," said Susan.

"Every soldier knows he might get killed," said Molly. "That's why every soldier is a hero."

"Yeah, but it seems to me that once they're killed, they just go to heaven, where everything is fine," said Linda. "It's the people left behind on earth who love them that have a harder time. They're sad, but they have to go on with the rest of their lives. I think Miss Campbell is as much a hero as her soldier was."

"But she can be proud of the sacrifice she made for her country," said Susan.

"I think I would be more sad than proud if my dad got killed," said Molly.

"Me, too," said Susan.

"Me, too," said Linda. "I'd sure rather be happy

and have the person I love home safe and sound than be proud because he died a hero."

"Yeah," said Molly. "Well, at least the war is supposed to be almost over. Our soldiers have pushed all the way into Germany. Mom says the Nazis have to surrender soon."

"I sort of don't get it," said Susan. "How do they decide when a war is over? Does one side change its mind and say it was wrong and then surrender?"

"No," said Linda. "A war is over when one side gives up because so many of its soldiers are killed it can't fight anymore."

"Oh," said Susan. "Well, it'll be great to have all the fighting end. I can hardly remember what it was like before the war. When it ends, everything will be wonderful."

"It seems like everything should be wonderful," said Linda. "But I don't see how it can be when so many people will be sad about their dads and friends and everyone who got killed or wounded."

"That's why our 'Hurray for the U.S.A.' show is so important," said Molly. "It's a way to show the wounded men that we're glad they are alive and to thank them for being so brave."

"That's right!" said Susan.

"It doesn't seem like very much, but I guess it's the best we can do," agreed Linda.

By now they were standing outside the drugstore. "Now, when we go in, you'd better let me do all the talking," said Susan, "because I know about the permanent."

"Okay," said Molly and Linda. They gave all their money to Susan, and she led them inside.

The shelves seemed fuller these days, now that there was less rationing. In the hair care section, there were lots of different shampoos and more than one kind of home permanent kit. Susan read one of the boxes. It said, "Big, Beautiful, Bouncy Curls for the New You."

"Oh, this is definitely the one we want," Susan said. "So you can be the New You. The New Molly."

"Better get the extra-strong formula," said Linda, "because Molly has long hair."

As Susan was paying for the kit, the drugstore man said, "Does your mother know you're using this?"

"Oh, it's not for *me*," said Susan innocently. "It's for

someone . . . older." That was true. Molly's birthday was two months before Susan's.

The three girls rushed out of the store and hurried back to Molly's house. They had decided to give Molly the permanent wave in their secret hide-out, the room above the garage.

Susan dragged a rickety old chair into the middle of the room. "Here," she said to Molly. "Sit on this. It'll be just like a beauty parlor." She wrapped a dusty sheet around Molly's shoulders.

"Some beauty parlor! For one thing, it's freezing cold up here," shivered Linda. "And how are you going to shampoo her hair? We don't have any water."

"Oh, we can skip that part," said Susan. She began to unbraid Molly's hair.

"No, we can't skip it," said Linda. "It says right here on the box: 'First, shampoo hair.'"

"That's probably only if your hair is dirty," said Susan. "Molly's hair is pretty clean already. Gosh, it sure is straight, Molly! And it's kind of long. Maybe we should cut it a little bit, so the curlers can hold it better."

Molly felt nervous. She began to suspect Susan

didn't really know what she was doing. "I think we'd better not cut my hair," she said. "If we did, Mom would be really mad."

"Okay," said Susan. "I don't have any scissors anyway. Now let's see. I guess it's time to put the waving lotion on your hair." She opened the bottle of lotion. A terrible smell filled the room.

"P.U.!" exclaimed Linda. "That stuff smells awful!"

"It smells like a wet dog!" said Molly. "I don't want to smell like *that*!"

"Oh, for heaven's sake!" said Susan. "If you want curls, you're just going to have to put up with the smell. I'm sure it wears off after a while."

"Maybe this bottle of lotion has gone bad or something," said Linda. She was pinching her nose between two fingers. "Did the waving lotion Gloria used smell like this?"

"I don't know," said Susan.

"You don't know? Weren't you there when she gave herself the permanent?" asked Molly.

"Not *exactly*," said Susan. "I didn't watch her do the whole thing. I saw her with the curlers in her hair, and I saw her after, when she took the curlers out."

"Susan!" groaned Molly. "You don't know how to do this at all, do you?"

"Of course I do," snapped Susan. "Anybody can read the directions on the box and kind of figure it out as you go along."

"Oh, brother!" said Linda. "Molly's probably going to end up bald!"

"She will not—" Susan began.

Just then, the door swung open and Jill burst in. "What are you guys doing up here?" she asked.

"Uh, just playing," said Molly. "What are you doing up here?"

"I came to . . ." said Jill. She stopped talking and sniffed the air. "Gosh! It reeks in here! What are you doing?" She looked at Molly sitting in the chair with her hair down. Then she frowned and squinted at Molly. "Molly McIntire, it smells like permanent wave lotion in here. You're not letting Linda and Susan give you a permanent, are you?"

Molly, Linda, and Susan were silent.

"Don't do it, Molly," said Jill. "Really, it's not that easy to do it right, and it'll look horrible if it comes out wrong. You'll regret it, you really will."

"But I *need* curly hair," wailed Molly. "I have to have it for the show, and for Dad, and everything. I just absolutely have to."

Jill sighed. "A permanent isn't the way to get curls. With hair like yours, it will just give you wrinkles and frizz. Listen, I can understand why you want to look good. I'll even help you. I'll set your hair every night between now and the show if that's what you want. I promise."

"Really?" asked Molly.

"Really," said Jill.

Molly was relieved. "Gee," she said. "Thanks, Jill. That will be much better."

"Yeah," said Linda. "We sort of knew we were getting in over our heads with this permanent business. Get it?"

Even Susan had to laugh. Molly was very glad the hair-raising experience was over.

# The New Molly

 unday night, Jill and Molly began work on the New Molly. Molly didn't even have to remind Jill of her promise. After dinner, Jill said, "Come on, Molly. Let's go up to my room."

"What are you two drips up to?" asked Ricky.

"None of your beeswax," answered Molly as she followed Jill upstairs.

Molly sat perfectly still on the stool at Jill's vanity table. Jill draped a towel around Molly's shoulders and undid her braids, brushing out the tangles with long, smooth strokes. She took a few strands and wrapped them around her hand, trying to make them curve under. They just flopped.

Molly sighed. "See?" she said. "It's hopeless."

"No, it's not," said Jill. "We'll set it in pin curls. It'll be fine."

Slowly and patiently, Jill twisted strands of hair into curlicues and pinned the curlicues with criss-crossed bobby pins. The curlicues were so tight that Molly's scalp felt as if someone were pulling her hair. The bald spots in between pin curls felt bare and cold. But Molly didn't dare make a peep of complaint. First of all, Jill might get mad and stop. Second of all, maybe it *had* to hurt for it to work.

Jill was quite expert. She held the twisted hair with one hand and opened the bobby pins by pulling them apart with her front teeth. Molly watched her in the mirror. Dad was right. Jill *was* very pretty and sophisticated-looking.

"Jill, how did you learn how to do all this stuff?" asked Molly.

"Oh, my friend Dolores taught me how to set hair ages ago," said Jill. "Tilt your head a little bit forward so I can reach the hair near your neck."

"I don't mean just how to set hair," said Molly. "I mean, how come your shirt always stays tucked in? And how come your elbows aren't scabby? And your socks wrinkle just right? How did you learn to look so sophisticated, like Dad said in his letter?" Molly was kind of afraid Jill might laugh, but she didn't.

"I don't know," said Jill. "I guess it comes naturally when you get older."

Molly sighed. "Even if I wore your exact same clothes, I still wouldn't look grown-up."

"You can't make it happen faster than it's going to happen," said Jill. "And you shouldn't try, anyway." She met Molly's eyes in the mirror. "Sometimes I'm sorry because I think the war made all of us grow up too fast. We had to kind of hurry into being serious. And I feel cheated, because Dad missed seeing us through some of the parts of being kids. He wasn't here to teach Brad how to ride a two-wheeler or to help me with algebra. I think you're lucky. At least you have a few more years of being a kid with him."

"I never thought of it that way," said Molly. "I want Dad to think I've changed, that I'm *not* just a dumb kid anymore."

Jill thought a moment. "Even if you don't look different, you *have* changed," she said.

"Really?" asked Molly. "I have? Like how, for instance?"

"Well," said Jill, "the most obvious thing is that you

*want* to be different. Gosh, you used to always want everything to be the same as before the war, which was really childish because things can't ever stay the same, especially when there's a war. Remember the fight we had about decorating the Christmas tree? You just wouldn't admit Christmas was going to have to be different with Dad away. This year you were more willing to change."

Jill opened up another bobby pin with her teeth and then went on thoughtfully, "And you don't clomp around the house the way you used to all the time. You're quieter. And I thought you grew up a lot and learned to think about other people when Emily came to stay with us. You were very generous with her. You definitely act more grown-up now than you did before."

"But I want to *look* grown-up," said Molly.

"Okay," Jill laughed. "That's what we're working on here! But I still think Dad will mostly care that you act older. You really do act more mature."

"Mature!" Molly was terribly flattered. "Mature" was one of Jill's highest words of praise. The opposite—"immature"—was her harshest criticism. Molly sat up very straight. It made her proud that Jill thought she was mature.

"You're done," said Jill. "Try not to wiggle around too much when you sleep or the bobby pins will fall out."

"Okay," said Molly. "Thanks a lot, Jill." She walked slowly down the hall to her bedroom, holding her neck stiff, as if she were balancing a bowl of water on her head.

Suddenly, Ricky jumped in front of her. "Help! Save us!" he shrieked. "It's a porcupine monster from outer space!" He clutched his head and pretended to faint from fear at the sight of her.

Molly was about to sock him. Then she thought of what Jill had said and stopped herself. She just kept walking and sighed, "How immature," leaving Ricky slumped against the wall behind her.

Sleeping on pin curls was like sleeping on thorns. Molly tried putting her face in the pillow, but then she couldn't breathe. She tried wadding up her pillow under her neck instead of under her head, but that made her neck hurt. The bobby pins seemed to find a way to dig into her scalp no matter what she did.

The next morning Molly's head was groggy from no sleep. Her scalp was sore. Her neck was stiff. She had funny red wrinkles on her face and marks from the bobby pins pressed into her cheeks. But it was all worth it, because when Jill took the bobby pins out, Molly's hair was—NOT STRAIGHT.

"Oh, Jill!" exclaimed Molly. "It's wonderful!"

Jill pursed her lips and studied Molly's hair with a critical eye. "We'll try it a different way tonight," she said. "This is okay, but it's more ripply than curly."

But Molly was very pleased with her new look. And at school, all the girls oohed and ahhed when she pushed back the hood on her jacket. She hadn't worn her hat. She was afraid it would crush her hair. So her ears were pink with both cold *and* pleasure when Susan said, "Gosh, Molly! You look like a movie star!"

Linda didn't go that far, but even she had a compliment. "If you took off your glasses, you'd look at least twelve years old, maybe even thirteen," she said seriously.

All day long, Molly was careful not to move her head too much. Every few moments, she'd reach back to touch the ripples with her fingers, to be sure they were still there. Her hair stayed ripply right up to the time for tap dance class. When Miss LaVonda saw her, she smiled. "Why, Molly! Don't you look darling!" Molly's heart lifted.

This was the week everyone got to try out to be Miss Victory. That day, Alison Hargate did the special dance first. Linda and Molly watched as Alison walked up the bleacher steps to take her position before the music started. The Miss Victory costume fit her perfectly. Alison's hair was so blond and her eyes were so blue, she seemed to glow and light up the stage even without the spotlights shining on her.

"Gee, she looks great, doesn't she?" whispered Molly.

Linda shrugged.

When the music started, the girls who were stars and stripes sang and danced their parts without a mistake. But Alison started the solo too late and had to hurry down the bleacher steps, so she was out of step with the music. Her feet seemed to get all tangled up. As she danced on, she did better, but she seemed very glad when the music was finally over.

Linda poked Molly and rolled her eyes. "She may

look good, but she sure can't dance as well as you can," she said.

Miss LaVonda made them all do the whole dance over and over while other girls tried out for the solo. Molly danced better every time. Having the ripples bounce up and down on her back felt wonderful. There was only one problem. As she danced, she got more sweaty, and the ripples began to unravel and droop in a discouraged way. By the end of class, the beautiful ripples had pretty much disappeared, and Molly was left with a scraggly mess of straight, sticky hair.

Unfortunately, the same thing happened every day. It didn't matter what Jill did to curl Molly's hair. She tried twisting it around rags, rolling it up in a hair net, gooing it up with cream, and drenching it with hair lacquer. When Molly woke up in the morning, she would have waves, ripples, and even curls. But as soon as she danced, her hair would straighten itself out and hang as limp as wet noodles. In the war against her hair, Molly was losing. And she was sure she'd never get to be Miss Victory unless she and Jill could find a way to make the curls stay curly.

Finally, it was Friday night, the night before

Molly's turn to try out to be Miss Victory. She and
Jill were desperate. "Okay," said Jill, as if she were a
general preparing for an all-out attack on the enemy.
"There's one last thing to try—the wet hair method."
Jill wet Molly's hair, twisted it up into tight pin curls,
then wet it again. Molly had to sleep with a towel over
her pillow, her hair was so wet. The next morning,
Molly went off to tap dance class with her damp hair
still in the pin curls. "Don't take the bobby pins out
until the very last minute," warned Jill.

It was a bitterly cold day. Molly was afraid the pin
curls would freeze solid as she hurried along the sidewalk. Her whole head felt like an ice cube. But when
she got to class and carefully took out all the pins, her
hair had dried and she had glorious, wavy curls. Susan
helped her fasten the Miss Victory star on her head.

"Oh, Molly!" Susan gasped. "You look absolutely
perfect!"

Molly looked in the mirror. She couldn't help smiling. She did look perfect, except for one thing—her
glasses. She took them off and put them inside one
of her regular shoes. She knew the dance so well, she
wouldn't need those glasses. Anyway, they belonged

to the old Molly, not this new, sophisticated Molly dressed in the gorgeous, sparkly Miss Victory costume.

Molly took her place at the top of the bleacher steps as the music began. Everything was a little fuzzy in front of her, but that just made it easier to imagine there was a big crowd watching her. Molly pretended that in the very front row, smiling and clapping, was the most important person of all: Dad.

At exactly the right moment, Molly danced down the steps in perfect time with the music. She danced better than she ever had before. It was as if the music was in her feet, making them light, moving them along through all the fancy steps without a bit of effort from Molly. After the dance, all the girls clapped and cheered for Molly. Linda and Susan clapped the loudest.

"Well!" said Miss LaVonda. "It seems we all agree that Molly should be Miss Victory. Congratulations, Molly! You did a fine job!"

She handed Molly a small plaid suitcase with a silver buckle. "You may use this suitcase to carry the Miss Victory costume back and forth from home to class. Take good care of that costume. You've certainly earned the privilege of wearing it!"

All the girls clapped again, and Molly heard Susan cheer, "Hurray for Molly! Molly is Miss Victory!" Molly thought it was probably the most perfect moment she'd ever had in her life—so far.

# The Show Must Go On

ust one more week until Dad comes home! Just one more week until the show! That was all Molly could think about. She was so happy, she danced everywhere, all the time. She danced along the sidewalk on the way to school. She danced in the lunch line. She danced off to rehearsals. She danced sitting down at the dinner table. Her feet were so full of excitement, she just couldn't keep them still.

"Olly Molly, you have turned into a jumping bean," her mother said early in the week. "You never stop moving."

"I can't help it, Mom," said Molly.

Mom shook her head and smiled. "I know how you feel. Whenever I think about Dad coming home, I feel all fluttery with excitement, too. I just don't show it as much. Your face is all pink with it!" She brushed

Molly's bangs from her forehead, then she frowned. "You're a bit feverish, dear. Do you feel all right?"

"Sure!" said Molly. Her throat was a little sore, but she figured that was from singing so much during rehearsals for the show.

Mom stared at Molly. "Your eyes look funny, too—as if you're coming down with something. I don't want you to go to bed with wet hair anymore this week. Is that understood? You'll catch a terrible cold."

"But, Mom—" Molly began.

"But, Molly," Mom said. "You don't want to be sick, do you?"

"No, but—"

"No buts about it. No more wet hair until right before the show. That's that," said Mom firmly.

When Mom sounded like that, there was no point in arguing. So Molly had to go back to her boring old braids for the rest of the week. Actually, it was kind of a relief. Molly's nose was sort of runny. She was afraid she *might* be catching a cold. Besides, her scalp needed a rest from being a prickly cactus.

But Saturday, the day before the show, there was going to be a dress rehearsal. Miss LaVonda said they would practice the whole show in their costumes, just like the real thing. So Mom let Molly sleep with wet hair Friday night and keep her pin curls damp on Saturday morning. "Wear a hat," Mom warned as they all got ready to go to the rehearsal. "Or you'll have icicles dangling down your back instead of curls!"

Molly, Linda, and Susan felt lucky that their act was last because that meant they'd be able to watch almost the whole show while they waited to go on-stage. There was a lot of confusion before the dress rehearsal finally began. The three girls sat in their seats watching Miss LaVonda herd all the nervous participants into their places.

The show began with Alison's mother, Mrs. Hargate, singing "The Star-Spangled Banner." She wore a fancy dress made out of shimmery green material. It draped around her, leaving one shoulder bare.

"Gee whiz, she looks like the Statue of Liberty in that dress," whispered Linda. "Do you think she chose it on purpose?"

Mrs. Hargate stretched out the high notes so much, the windows seemed to shake. It made Molly's throat hurt just to listen. "Poor Alison," murmured Susan.

"I'd die of embarrassment if *my* mother sang like that in front of all my friends."

Everyone in the auditorium, especially Alison, relaxed with a sigh when Mrs. Hargate finally sang, "And the hooooooooome of the braaaaaaaave!" But Mrs. Hargate looked very pleased as she walked slowly off the stage.

The next act was more lively. It was the Jefferson Junior High School Band. "Look! There's Ricky with the rest of the tubas!" Molly said to Linda and Susan. Ricky and the other tuba players turned their tubas from side to side as they played so that the huge, shiny horns flashed gold under the spotlights. After the band, some little kids gave a skit about buying War Bonds. Brad was in the skit. He held up a big sign that said "BUY."

Next, the mayor of Jefferson spoke. At the end of his speech, he introduced Mrs. McIntire, who asked people to donate blood to the Red Cross Blood Drive. Molly held her handkerchief up to her nose the whole time her mother was speaking. She was afraid she might sneeze and make her mother forget what she was supposed to say. But she needn't have worried.

Mrs. McIntire seemed very calm up on the stage. She gave her message in a loud, clear voice, and then she sat down.

"Your mom was great!" said Linda.

"Sure," said Molly as she blew her nose. She was proud of her mother. Dad would be proud and surprised, too. Before the war, Mom would have been much too shy to make a speech. Now she thought nothing of it.

The church choir sang hymns next. Jill was in the choir, but Molly couldn't stay to listen. She and Linda and Susan had to go backstage to put on their costumes. Molly was very glad to take the bobby pins out of her hair because her head ached so badly. But as she pinned the shiny crown to her glorious curls, she forgot all about her headache. She shivered with excitement and anticipation.

"Here goes!" whispered Linda as she and the other stars and stripes took their places.

The audience gasped, "Oh!" when the curtain went up and the giant flag of dancing girls filled the stage. And when Molly danced down the bleacher steps in her sparkly Miss Victory costume, the audience burst into loud, excited applause. They whooped and cheered and sang along with the music.

Molly couldn't actually see the audience without her glasses, but she could hear them and feel their happy enthusiasm. She danced and twirled and tapped and spun, doing every step perfectly, in a sort of haze of happiness. When she was through, everyone in the audience stood up and cheered for a long time. They kept on cheering even after the curtain was lowered, so the stagehands raised the curtain again. All the girls took another bow.

When the curtain finally came down and stayed down, Miss LaVonda rushed out onto the stage and hugged Molly. "You looked perfect and you danced perfectly!" she said. "The audience loved you! And this wasn't even the real audience. If you do as well tomorrow, you'll bring down the house!"

Molly beamed. She wasn't exactly sure what Miss LaVonda meant about "bringing down the house," but she figured it was a good thing for an act to do. She couldn't wait until the next night. Miss LaVonda would see: Molly would dance even *better* when Dad was in the audience!

It was late when the McIntires got home from the rehearsal. Molly was very, very tired all over. Her head felt heavy. It was hard to hold it up while Jill set her hair in wet pin curls before they went to bed. Molly felt weak and shivery. *I am NOT sick,* she said to herself. *I'm just tired. I'll be fine tomorrow, because tomorrow is the day Dad's coming home. TOMORROW!*

But Molly's head still felt heavy the next morning when she woke up. Her throat was sore. Her nose was completely stuffed up. Every time she swallowed, her ears hurt. Every muscle ached. *I'll feel better after breakfast,* Molly thought as she dragged herself out of bed.

But she could only pick at her breakfast. It hurt too much to swallow. She was sipping her orange juice very, very slowly when Brad burst into the kitchen. He was dressed in his best suit. "Can you tie my tie for me, Mom?" he asked.

"Why, Brad!" exclaimed Mrs. McIntire as she turned from the sink. "Don't you look handsome! But isn't it a little early to be dressed up for the show?"

"I'm dressed up for Dad," said Brad.

"Well, I don't think Dad will be here until late this afternoon, if he gets here at all today," said Mrs.

McIntire. "We still haven't heard from him yet."

"I want to be ready no matter what," said Brad.

Molly and Mrs. McIntire laughed. "All right," said Mom. "But remember, this is your only good suit. Put your napkin in your collar so you don't spill on it. You'll have to stay tidy all day."

Then Mrs. McIntire turned to Molly and said, "I know you're excited, too, about Dad *and* the show, Molly. But you've got to eat your breakfast. You can't dance on an empty stomach."

"I'm just not hungry," said Molly.

"Not hungry?" said Mom. She immediately put her hand on Molly's forehead. "Molly! You're burning up with fever! Oh, I never should have allowed this wet hair nonsense! Come back upstairs with me. I'm going to take your temperature."

"I'm *not* sick, Mom," protested Molly. Her voice sounded hoarse. "I'm sure I don't have a temperature."

"We'll see," said Mom as she led Molly upstairs.

It turned out that Molly did have a temperature, a high one. "Oh, no," murmured Mrs. McIntire as she looked at the thermometer. "One hundred and three degrees. You'd better get back into your pajamas, dear.

Why don't you get into my bed to rest? I'm going to call the doctor."

By now Molly felt so sick she was almost glad to get into Mom's bed and rest her cheek on the cool pillow. *It's probably a good idea to sleep a lot this morning,* she thought. *That way I'll be in good shape for the show this afternoon.*

When the doctor came, he asked Molly to say "ahh" as he looked down her throat. Then he looked into her ears and frowned. "Hmph!" he said. "You've got a very bad ear infection, young lady. You'll have to take this medicine three times a day. And get plenty of sleep. I'll come to see you tomorrow."

Mrs. McIntire followed the doctor into the hallway. Molly could hear them talking softly together outside the door. Then Mrs. McIntire came back in and sat on the bed.

"Well, Molly," Mom said sadly, "the doctor says you *must* stay in bed until the fever goes away. He says you can't go anywhere today."

Molly sat up. "Mom," she said, "I'll stay in bed as much as you want after the show. I promise. But I have to get up this afternoon. I can't be sick in bed when

Dad comes home. And I've absolutely *got* to be in the show. I'm Miss Victory."

Mom sighed. "I'm sorry, dear. I can't allow you to be in the show. You're just too sick. I'll have to call Miss LaVonda and tell her she has to find someone else to take your part."

Molly felt too terrible to protest anymore. She rolled over and buried her face in the pillow. Mom rubbed her back. "I know how disappointed you are," she said. "I'm so sorry this happened, today of all days. I can't think of anything that would be more sad for you, and I can't think of anything to say to make it better." She was quiet for a while, then she said, "Try to get some rest," and left to call Miss LaVonda.

Molly hunched herself into a ball. All of her ached with sickness and sadness and awful disappointment. All of her hopes, all of her wonderful plans, *everything* was ruined! Finally, she couldn't help it. She began to cry. She cried until she fell asleep.

A long time later, in the afternoon, she woke up when someone opened the door to the bedroom. It was Ricky.

"Hi," he said glumly. "Guess what? We just got this

telegram from Dad. Here, look." He tossed the yellow telegram to Molly. It said

> *Travel plans changed. Don't know when I'll*
> *get there, but will be later than expected.*
> *Can't wait to see you.*
>     *Love, Dad*

Molly didn't say anything. She just handed the telegram to Ricky and sank back against the pillows. *Now Dad isn't even coming,* she thought. *Nothing is working out. Absolutely nothing.*

"So," said Ricky with a sigh, "you don't have to get all upset about Dad missing you in the show because you're sick. He won't see *any* of us in the show because he won't be there. It stinks, doesn't it?" He kicked the door with his sneaker. "But Mom keeps saying, 'The show must go on!' So we're all going over to the auditorium later. Mrs. Gilford is coming here to take care of you. I'm supposed to ask if you want anything now."

Molly shook her head no.

"Okay," said Ricky. "Oh, I almost forgot. I'm also supposed to get your Miss Victory costume to bring with us."

"It's all in that suitcase by the closet in my room," said Molly. She thought about how proud she'd felt when Miss LaVonda gave her the suitcase with the costume in it. "Who gets to be Miss Victory?"

"Alison," said Ricky. "I guess because she looks so good in the costume. But everyone knows she's not half as good a dancer as you are," he blurted out. As he hurried out the door, he bumped into Jill.

"I brought your paper dolls and your kaleidoscope," said Jill. "I thought you might be bored up here."

"Thanks," said Molly. Her voice was so hoarse it was a whisper.

"I wish I were the one who was sick," said Jill. "I really do. I'm just in the choir. No one would miss me in the show. But you! You worked so hard to learn that Miss Victory dance and to get your hair just right. It isn't fair. You must be so disappointed."

"Yeah," croaked Molly. "But I'm even more disappointed about Dad not coming home."

"I know," said Jill. "It's very hard to be mature about disappointments like this." She sighed. "I guess

I'd better get ready to go. See you later."

After the door was closed, Molly began to yank the bobby pins out of her hair one by one. There was no reason, no reason at all, for curls *now*. Her damp, defeated hair felt like wet snakes, so she braided it up any old which way, just to get it off her shoulders. *Same dumb braids,* she thought. *I'm the same dumb me.* But who cared? There was no reason to be the New Molly anymore. Besides, if she had not been so stupid about curls, she wouldn't have caught cold in the first place. It was her own stupidity that had ruined everything.

In a little while, Mom came in with a glass of ginger ale and some medicine. She looked beautiful and smelled like perfume. "We've got to hurry off to the show now," she said. "I'm sorry to leave you alone, but Mrs. Gilford missed the bus. She'll be here in about half an hour. And we'll all be home after the show, at about six o'clock. Try to sleep." She kissed Molly on the cheek and squeezed her hand. "I'm really very sorry about all this, dear," she said. And then she left.

The house was quiet after everyone had gone. Molly played with her paper dolls for a while and looked through the kaleidoscope, but she couldn't get interested in either one. A cheerless dusk filled the room. Molly switched on the light. *Probably the only light on in the house,* she thought gloomily. She felt lonely and very, very sorry for herself. No show. No Miss Victory. And worst of all, no Dad. She had thought everything was going to be so perfect. Perfect, huh! Perfectly awful was more like it.

And on top of all that, her ears ached and buzzed and didn't even work right. Right now, for instance, she thought she heard the front door opening. But it couldn't be, because it was too soon for Mrs. Gilford and way too soon for everyone to come home from the show. Now she thought she heard someone climbing up the stairs. Dumb ears!

"I'm home!" a voice called out.

It was Dad.

"Dad!" gasped Molly. She pulled back the covers and sprang out of bed. "Dad! Dad! You're home!" She tore out of the room and ran halfway down the stairs, right into Dad's arms. She hugged him so hard his hat fell off and tumbled down the steps. Her nose was squashed against his coat, but she didn't care.

Without a word, Dad hugged Molly for a long, long

time. Then he put his hands on her shoulders and just stared at her. Finally he said, "Gosh and golly, olly Molly! You look exactly as I remembered you, just as I've pictured you for two long years. You look perfect!"

Molly grinned. "Perfect!" she said. Then she hugged Dad again.

Absolutely perfect.

# INSIDE Molly's World

World War Two ended in 1945, and times changed for all Americans—including young girls like Molly. Thousands of families were reunited when fathers, brothers, and sons returned from the fighting. Cheering crowds met the ships that brought troops back home. They welcomed the soldiers as heroes. People believed that the whole world would be a better place because American soldiers had fought and helped win the war.

As Americans' lives returned to normal, the things that had been scarce during the war became plentiful again. Factories that had made guns, bullets, and tanks for fighting went back to making refrigerators, washing machines, and bicycles. People bought these new things quickly because their old ones had worn out during the war. Factories also made things that most Americans had never owned before, like cars and television sets.

During the war, men left their jobs to become soldiers and women went to work in factories doing any work that needed to be done. But after the war, most women stopped working. They saw posters that told them it was patriotic to give their jobs back to the men. Magazines said that women's most important work was caring for children, cooking, and keeping a clean house. Young women were encouraged to marry young. So many couples started families that the period was called "the baby boom."

Though the war was over, it had been a terrible experience that changed the lives of people everywhere. The war was especially devastating for people who lived near the fighting. Women, children, and old people were killed by bombs, disease, and starvation. London, England, where Emily lived, was a dangerous place during the war. Starting in 1940, German bombs fell on the city almost every night. In addition to the damage caused by the bombs, there were shortages of food and clothing, and both were severely rationed.

Many English children were *evacuated* from, or moved out of, London to keep them safe. Sometimes mothers and children moved to the countryside to live with family or friends. But many children were sent away from London without their parents, traveling by ship to Australia, Canada, or the United States as Emily was. Families had no idea how long they would be separated, and children had to learn to be as brave as soldiers.

After the war, *refugees*—people whose homes had been destroyed—didn't have food, clothing, or places to live. Whole cities needed to be rebuilt. Americans wanted all people's lives to return to normal, so the United States took the lead in helping its allies, as well as its enemies, build their countries back up again.

When the war ended and families all over the world were reunited, it sometimes took a while for them to get to know one another again. But of all the changes the war brought, readjusting to normal, safe lives at home in peacetime was surely the most welcome change of all.

# Read more of MOLLY'S stories,

available from booksellers and at *americangirl.com*

## ❧ *Classics* ❧

*Molly's classic series, now in two volumes:*

*Volume 1:*
### A Winning Spirit
Life on the home front is full of challenges. Molly does her best to make do with less and help the war effort. Missing Dad, who is far away in England, is the hardest sacrifice of all!

*Volume 2:*
### Stars, Stripes, and Surprises
Even allies have arguments sometimes. Molly learns to get along with new friends, as well as forever friends, with some surprises along the way.

## ❧ *Journey in Time* ❧

*Travel back in time—and spend a day with Molly!*

### Chances and Changes
Take a trip to Camp Gowonagin with Molly! Go on an over night nature hike, compete in the swim meet, and discover fun camp traditions. Choose your own path through this multiple-ending story.

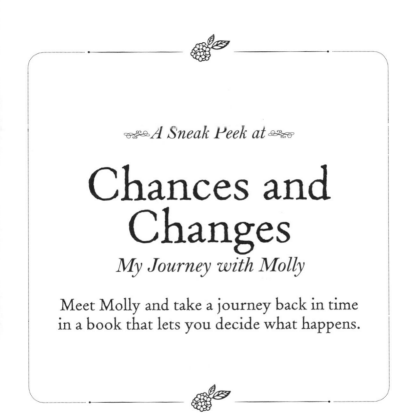

*A Sneak Peek at*

# Chances and Changes

*My Journey with Molly*

Meet Molly and take a journey back in time
in a book that lets you decide what happens.

t's just before seven a.m. when my dog, Barney, and I race through the woods. My best friend, Bea, is waiting for me at the edge of the pasture, and she practically drags me to the barn, putting her hand over my eyes just as we walk in.

When Bea takes her hands away from my eyes, she says, "You can look now."

It's dark in the barn, so at first all I see is a shaft of sunlight. Then my eyes adjust and I see Bea's horse, Aurora, and—"Oh!" I gasp. "Aurora had her foal!"

"She sure did," says Gem. "And he's perfectly healthy." Gem—my grandmother—has helped at the births of hundreds of baby animals, both wild and tame. We live in Seneca Forest Preserve, and Gem is the wildlife ranger. "Bea called me at five this morning," says Gem. She's in the stall, stroking Aurora's sweaty neck. "But by the time I got here, Aurora had already done all the hard work."

Bea and I hug. We stand outside the stall staring at the foal, so enchanted and enthralled that we're silent. Aurora looks over her shoulder at us, then nudges her spindly-legged, shiny black foal as if to say, "Go meet the girls. They're my old friends." The foal wobbles. It can't quite figure out how to coordinate all four legs, which are as stiff and skinny as stilts, so it stands still, looking puzzled.

"Never mind," Bea tells the foal. "Stay put. We can admire you from here."

"Hello, Aurora's foal," I say. "Hello, Moon Shadow."

"Moon Shadow?" asks Gem

"That's the name we chose," I say.

"Margaret Maybe," Bea says, using her nickname for me. "Are you sure you're sure?"

I nod, and Bea looks at Gem. "We had a list of about a million others," Bea explains with a grin. "You know how Margaret is about making decisions."

I shrug and admit, "We talked about it for months, every day."

"And yesterday Margaret decided not to decide until we saw the foal," Bea laughs. "Well here he is. Now, every day, we can watch Moon Shadow grow."

Gem and I exchange a look. "Ah," Gem says gently. "You two need to talk."

My heart twists. "Bea," I say slowly. "I . . . I'm not sure I'll be here every day."

"How come?" asks Bea.

"I got a letter yesterday," I say. "I've been invited to a summer music camp. On a scholarship!"

"What?" Bea says. "How?"

"It was Mr. Speltz," I say, picturing our orchestra teacher. "He nominated me, and he sent the admissions committee a video of our concert."

As I explain my great opportunity, Bea's face loses its glow from Moon Shadow's arrival.

"When would you leave?" Bea asks.

"The end of next week."

"And when would you come home?"

I look at Gem. "In eight weeks," I say softly.

"Eight weeks? That's two months!" Bea's voice is full of dismay. "That's practically the whole summer!"

I try to say something but I can't. So I just nod.

"You can't go," Bea says passionately. "Aurora just had her foal. Moon Shadow is finally here, and we have plans, and I need your help."

I knew it. Bea is crushed.

"This is a wonderful opportunity for Margaret," Gem says kindly. "I'll be here, Bea. You know I'll help you any way I can."

Bea sighs sadly. "It won't be the same. And what

about you? Who will help you with the projects around the preserve?"

My breath catches. I hadn't thought of that. Does Gem need me to stay? Would she even admit it if she did?

"I'll be fine," says Gem. "Besides, Mischa's here three days a week. He can give me all the help I need."

Gem's words sting a bit. At the start of summer, Mischa swooped in from far-away California. He's a student at a nearby college and is doing an internship with Gem. He and I didn't exactly hit it off. He took over things I do without even asking me. I've done my best to stay far away from Mischa. I'm not interested in getting to know him the way Gem is. I can't wait until his internship is done and he leaves.

But Gem is still talking about me leaving. She says, "It's time for Margaret to take a chance and try something new. It's not forever."

"But it's right now. You'll miss so much of Moon Shadow's changes."

I look over at the stall, where Moon Shadow is nestled close to Aurora. My heart aches from seeing them—and from having to make this decision.

"I'll miss you," Bea whispers. "You're my best friend. What will I do without you?"

"I haven't decided yet," I say quickly. "Maybe I won't go."

Bea shakes her head. "Margaret Maybe," she says. She sounds so sad.

I meander through the woods alone, hoping to clear my head. Usually, when I've got a problem, I ask Gem or Bea for advice. But this time, they are part of my problem. Gem wants me to go to music camp. Bea wants me to stay home. Not only can't I decide what to do, but whatever I choice I make is going to disappoint one of them.

After walking for a long time, I flop down on some rotting wooden steps that I've never noticed before. The steps lead nowhere, which is appropriate because so far, my thinking's led nowhere, too. I'm a person who hates to make anyone unhappy, so I hate to make decisions and here I am, faced with a whopper.

One minute, I have this itchy urge to go and the next minute, I think, 'No way!'

Argh! When it comes to making this choice, I

choose not to!

There's a breeze in the treetops but the morning sun is getting hot. I glance at my watch to see how late it's getting and as I do, I see something shiny on the ground. It's jewelry, a gold pin with a green stone, probably dropped by a hiker. I pick it up and rub the dirt off the stone. Whoosh! First there's darkness, then glaring sunlight.

When my eyes can focus again, I see that the steps I'm sitting on aren't rotted anymore, and they lead up to a big wooden building behind me that's labeled: Mess Hall.

What just happened? Where did the building behind me come from, and how come the steps seem new? I look at the pin. Everything was normal until I rubbed the green stone. But before I can figure out what's happened, I hear a girl say, "Hi!"

Shoving the pin in my pocket, I look at her. I have to squint, because now the sun is glinting off the girl's eyeglasses. "Uh, hi?" I say, sounding jangled.

"You must be a new camper," the girl says. "Welcome to Camp Gowonagin." She flings her arms wide.

"Isn't it great?"

Camp what? Am I having some kind of camp
decision-making dream? Is this girl even real?

Then she smiles, and it's the most real smile I've
ever seen. "I'm Molly," she says. With old-fashioned
politeness, she holds out her hand to shake mine and
says, "How do you do? What's your name?"

"Margaret," I manage to mumble, wondering
where I am. There's no camp in Seneca Forest Preserve,
so I'm sure not home. I look around. Beside the Mess
Hall, a wide, shady path winds up a hill. There are
tan tents on one side of the hill and on the other side
green fields slope down to a border of dark green pine
trees. A sparkling lake peeks through the trees. Everywhere, I see chattering groups of girls. Most of them
are dressed like Molly, in white shirts, red shorts, and
red caps. A bus pulls up, more girls spill out. I grip the
steps for dear life because I am so dizzy. I realize that
impossible as it seems, somehow I have been transported to a girls' summer camp. How on earth did this
happen?

My face must look as mixed up and scared as I
feel, because Molly says kindly, "Camp is sort of

overwhelming at first, I know. But you'll love it! I promise. You'll feel at home soon. The camp director, Miss Butternut, is really nice and so are all the counselors." Her face brightens. "I know what!" she says. "I'll introduce you to my friend Linda. Wait here a second while I run inside the Mess Hall and get her."

Molly takes the steps two at a time, her long brown braids bouncing on her back as she bounds past me up the steps into the Dining Hall. As the screen door swings shut behind her, I slip my hand into my pocket, take out the pin, and look at it in the palm of my hand. What will happen if I rub it again? Will it take me home?

Unusually for me, I make an instant decision: I've got to find out. Quickly, I rub the pin again. And again, after a whoosh of darkness, I blink in the light and I'm back in my own woods, sitting on the weedy steps, the pin still in my hand. I look at my watch and gulp. No time has passed! I'm relieved to be home, but then I begin to think. I liked Molly. She was so friendly and cheery and welcoming. Being with her felt good: it was a break from worrying about the decision I have to make. Here's a golden opportunity to find out what it's like to go someplace new, I think. The part of me that itches for adventure wants to go back to Molly. As Gem would say, "Take a chance!" So even though I'm not sure where the pin will take me, I make another impulsive decision. I rub it again, hoping it will bring me back to Molly.

I whoosh though darkness, blink in bright sunshine, and hurray! I turn to see Molly and another girl in a camp uniform just like hers smiling at me as they come down the steps from the Mess Hall. I think it's probably safest to keep the pin a secret, so I put it back into my pocket again.

"This is Linda," says Molly. "And this," she says, patting my shoulder, "is our new friend. Her name is Margaret, like Princess Margaret in England."

"Also like Margaret Truman," says Linda. "President Harry Truman's daughter."

"President Truman," Molly says, shaking her head. "I still can't get used to saying that! The president has always been Franklin Roosevelt my whole life."

Whoa. This talk of princesses and presidents has

me completely confused. Who are they talking about? Truman is not the president. Not now! Then it hits me: I'm not just in another place; I'm in another time. The pin has transported me back to the past. Yikes! I sort of want to faint and I sort of want to cheer. I feel terrified and excited both at the same time.

Linda's asking me a question. "Don't you think it's unfair that President Roosevelt didn't live to see V-E Day, the end of the war in Europe?" she says.

I wrack my rattled brains, trying to remember my American history so that I can figure out what year I'm in. We learned that Franklin Roosevelt led our country out of the Great Depression in the 1930s and nearly to the end of World War II. Roosevelt died suddenly and his vice president, Harry Truman, took over. My heart thumps. Somehow, I have traveled back to 1945!

# About the Author

VALERIE TRIPP says that she became
a writer because of the kind of person she
is. She says she's curious, and writing
requires you to be interested in everything.
Talking is her favorite sport, and writing
is a way of talking on paper. She's a day-
dreamer, which helps her come up with
ideas. And she loves words. She even loves
the struggle to come up with the right
words as she writes and rewrites. Ms. Tripp
lives in Maryland with her husband.